THANE

Mystic Zodiac

Book 1

Brandy Walker

Thane, Mystic Zodiac
Copyright © 2015 Brandy Walker
Cover by TEZ Graphics, Brandy Walker
Image: © Viorel Sima | Dreamstime.com
Edited by Noel Varner

First Electronic Print, Jan 2015

QUOTE:

Everything I have dreamed of is at the tip of my fingers. I won't let this woman stand in my way. ~ Thane

BLURB

Fallen Angel Thane has been exiled to the realm of humans and Mystics for almost fifty years after what he considers a slight misunderstanding, too bad Zeus didn't agree. After the blush of exile wears off, Thane dedicates his new life to helping those in need, all in the hope of impressing the imposing God.

A visit from his Watcher with one more task sets Thane up to finally get what he's dreamed about for decades… his rightful place back on Olympus with his brothers. All he needs to do is keep one woman from "doing something stupid." He determined to ignore his body responding for the first time in almost fifty years in order to go home.

Amara Hope is desperate to bring her brother home, traveling into the heart of Viral City day after day putting her life at risk. As her last living relative, he's all she has left. When a hunky good samaritan grudgingly offers help, she's all too willing to accept. Once they get her brother home and begin spending more time together, the more Amara knows he's the one for her.

What the two don't know is that the Gods are playing games with their lives, and they're on a collision course with love.

NOTE: Mystic Zodiac is a 12 book series. It is NOT a serial. Each book ends in a happily ever after for the main couple. However, the prologue and epilogue of each story follows the Gods that kick off the series, Eros and Chlotho (aka Chloe). At the end of the series the bet between the two will come to a conclusion.

PROLOGUE

On a cold winter's day the Fates: Clotho (Chloe), Lachesis (Lacy), and Atropos (Rose), lazed in the Parthenon, listening to the other Gods and Goddesses singing each other's praise. Arrogant, pompous, buffoons who thought too much of the gifts they wielded over the humans and Mystics, beat their chests like primates in a show of dominance. It never changed on Mount Olympus.

As far as Chloe was concerned, no one would ever be above her and her sisters' station. Not even Zeus himself, though he liked to believe differently. She and her sisters were the ones deciding life, longevity, and death; determining the fate, as it were, of each individual on earth and beyond. She and her sisters should be the ones the other Gods and Goddesses revered and bowed down to. Feared with every fiber of their being.

Lounging on a gold tufted parlor chaise, Chloe eyed a group of women scurrying by. Tall, lithe, blonde-haired nymphs rushing to the entrance of the Parthenon, tripping over each other to be the first to reach whatever bobble-

1

headed goal they had. "This looks marginally interesting," she mumbled, nudging her sister Lacy awake.

Lacy yawned, blinking her owlish brown eyes. "What looks interesting, dear?"

With a long, thin finger, Chloe pointed to the group. They were surrounding someone who had just entered the room; a magnificent, golden-haired, cocky, pain in the ass God — to be exact.

Eros. A shiver of desire raced down her spine.

Lacy grunted before closing her eyes. "That's not interesting Chloe, that's Eros. The man is too full of himself for my taste."

"Yes," she murmured. "We both know you love a man who will kneel at your feet until you tell him otherwise."

That was not Chloe's idea of a man. She liked one who took what he wanted, when he wanted it. That man would have confidence and an edge or arrogance. All of which Eros had an abundance of. Yes, he was full of himself. She knew that. It didn't mean she couldn't lust after him though. She yearned to taste his full lips and feel his silky smooth skin beneath her hands. Run her fingers over the hard ridges of his abs. Dip below that flimsy excuse of a wrap stretched tight across his lean hips and hanging on by the grace of Zeus. He never was one to adhere to the typical clothing of the Greeks. He showed off his body for one and all, reveling in the stares filled with undisguised lust. She could appreciate that display, even though she couldn't stand him on any other level.

Chloe hungered for him the way one craved a decadent meal filled with rich meats, lush fruits, and flowing mead. Eros was a treat she wanted only to taste and have fill her body until she tipped over, drunk on pleasure. That was all. She had no plans to keep the man. Like everyone else, his fate was already sealed. He would eventually find the one woman he would forsake all others for. Lucky for her, that wouldn't happen any time soon.

The high-pitched shrieks and giggling of those annoying women skated across Chloe's ears as Eros sauntered by. He stood well above them, shining in all his glory. He tossed one of his "I'm beautiful and I know it" smiles her way, setting her teeth on edge. She couldn't help but seethe over the way he'd rejected her the week before. Brushed her aside for a dalliance with one of Zeus's prized nymphs. A dark-haired voluptuous woman rumored to be the naughtiest of lays, up for anything and able to pleasure a man for hours until she allowed him to go over the brink into sweet oblivion.

Chloe didn't consider herself to be the hag or old woman, regardless of her age, as mythology liked to claim. Like her sisters she was tall, thin, and strikingly beautiful. She knew women would kill to have her caramel-colored hair that fell softly in long waves down her back. Or possess her deep brown eyes men said they got lost in and lush red lips as sweet as ripened cherries.

Eros should be thankful she gave him a passing thought to be her lover. That she found him worthy of her time. He should kiss the ground she walked on just to be close to her. Grovel and beg for her attention.

But no, he did none of that. Instead, he had the audacity to laugh in her face as if her proposition were a joke. Did he not understand she could end his life with the snap of her fingers, immortal or not?

Rose roused from where she reclined next to her, a sour look painted on her pale face. "It's gotten too loud in here sisters. We will return home now."

"I agree," Lacy chimed in. "Let us leave this place with its — lower beings — making fools of themselves."

Chloe's sisters rose and began to move away. Slowly, she stood, smoothing out her dark blue chiton while getting a fill of Eros one last time. He threw his head back and laughed heartily at one of the insipid women before wrapping his arm around her shoulders and kissing her soundly. When he released her, his gaze collided with

3

Chloe's. The slow rise of the corner of his mouth set off her fury with him once again.

Without thought she stomped over to where he sprawled with his harem. "You think you are so wonderful, Eros. The pre-eminent gift to both man and woman. Using your looks and ability to arouse desire in those around you to get what you want. Other than for sexual entertainment, you're useless. Even your gift is a joke. You help mortals fall in love. How ridiculously easy that must be. Zeus knows, we wouldn't want to tax your limited abilities by giving you something that mattered."

The cavernous room fell silent. In one smooth movement, Eros rose from his seat. The women surrounding him gasped in unison before closing their silly mouths. He stood in front of Chloe, towering over her, before she had a chance to flee. Not that she would give him that particular satisfaction.

"Oh sweet, Chloe. Still hurt at being rebuffed?" His words came out on a purr. Hatred rose within her. The man oozed sensuality and used it to his advantage.

"Never," she hissed, knowing full well it was a complete and utter lie. Eros had to have figured as much. He lips lifted, a smirk spreading across his face as he stepped closer. She could feel the heat of his body, though there were still many inches between them. The thin film of her dress did nothing to diminish that heat or stop her body from wanting to melt into him.

"I believe you are," he stated, regarding her in study.

She pressed her lips together to keep her words at bay. He would use whatever she said against her. It's how he liked to play. How most Gods liked to get their rocks off. His head tilted to the side, a thoughtful look smoothing his features.

Damn the man for being gorgeous.

"I have a game for you, a challenge if you will. One I think you'll quite enjoy."

"There is no game I want to play with you, Eros. That momentary lapse in judgment has passed," she said with feigned disinterest.

He stepped forward, closing the distance between them. Chloe sucked in a sharp breath as his chest brushed against hers. Her nipples responding on contact, hardening to rigid points.

"You would never pass up a challenge, I know you too well. Besides, this one has quite a wicked reward if you prevail. Something you desperately want and I denied."

A flash of arousal burst through her. Her sex throbbed in reaction. He couldn't mean what she thought. She knew what she had been denied and though she would not admit it to him, she still wanted it—wanted him. She licked her lips and watched as his eyes dilated, tracking the movement. He wasn't as immune to her as he portrayed.

She was unable to resist now that she knew. "I do love a challenge," she whispered. She raked his body with a gaze; so lost in him, she jumped when he slipped an arm around her waist, pressing her into him. Her body betrayed her fake lack of interest in him by quivering in response.

"I challenge you to match twelve couples."

She opened her mouth to retort how easy that would be, when his finger landed on her lips, silencing the words that had yet to come out.

"Not until I'm done. Twelve couples, one a month, but they won't only be human. I deal with much more than you think. You, my sweet Chloe, will match one Mystic a month for the next year, following the signs of the Mystic Zodiac. They must fall in love—no—declare their love to one another. If you succeed, as you surely believe you will, then you get me. For one...whole...month."

He dropped his finger from her lips, his arm from around her waist, and took a step back. She nearly

5

stumbled, locking her knees before that happened.

"An entire month?" she croaked, her mouth having gone dry. Gods…the things she could do to him in a month's time.

He grinned like a fool. "Yes. All to yourself. No other playthings to occupy my time. Only you. Would that satisfy you?"

The young maiden within urged her to say yes. The wizened woman inside cautioned her. How could she lose though? Helping humans and Mystics fall in love couldn't be that difficult. Humans fell in love too easily and too often. Mystics, if they had been on that realm long enough, did as well. It would be a breeze.

"Will I be choosing the Mystic or will you?"

"I will, of course. It is my job to know who will fall and when. I do have more than just one couple a month to deal with. I'll give you the names, you'll figure out the how. It isn't all bows and arrows anymore. Times have changed, as have people. Consider it an added degree of difficulty, since you find my job so easy. If you're successful, we'll meet again on the first day of the next month and I'll give you the next couple. If you aren't successful, that is where the challenge ends."

The deal sounded wonderful in her head and too good to be true. There had to be a catch. Something he got out of it if she failed. No God or Goddess did anything without a return in kind. "What will I owe you? If, by chance, I'm unsuccessful."

Eros grinned. "That's just it. You'll owe me. One favor of my choosing. Doesn't matter what it is, you'll have to deliver."

Chloe pursed her lips and thought it over. It didn't take long to come to a decision. Confidence was never something she lacked. "You have a deal Eros — and you better be worth it."

Eros threw his head back and laughed, much like he had earlier. When his laughter died down, he stared at her with a twinkle in his eyes. "Oh, I am Chloe. I am definitely worth it." Quick as lightning, he dropped a soft kiss on her lips. "I'll call on you tomorrow." He spun away, joining the women back on the lush pillow-laden seating on the floor.

Chloe crossed her arms over her breasts, hiding her body's reaction to him. The fools around her didn't need to know of her attraction. "Your challenge has been accepted. Give me the name," she demanded.

Eros chuckled, spreading his arms out to encompass the women around him. "I'm done for now. I have other pursuits to attend to. You can wait, Chloe, or are you that desperate to have me?"

"No one would ever be desperate over you. You give yourself freely to one and all."

He pinned her with a look that stole her breath. Eyebrow raised, lips thinned. She stepped too far in pushing him. He opened his mouth and she cut him off.

"Tomorrow then," she snapped. Turning on her heel, she left as quickly as she could without making more of a scene. His voice didn't ring out behind her with the truth, and for that she was grateful.

"Blast, the damn man for being gracious."

*****

Eros pounded on the heavy wooden door of The Fates' home, hoping his visit would be quick. A small part of him was still pissed about the day before. He did not fall into bed with any and everybody, regardless of the rumors swirling around his name.

Great thought went into selecting his paramours. What they could do for him or to him? Was the risk worth the reward? Did he want more than a simple dalliance?

The second those words were out of her sensual mouth; he should have demanded they meet at the Parthenon, or the court at Zeus's dwelling. Neutral territory with plenty of onlookers would eliminate words of foul play later. It would also hold him in check. His lust for the woman raged within and make him reckless. The knowledge that every word and action was being watched, his only saving grace.

It was too late to alter things now. They were on a collision course with passion.

A small gust of cold air whipped past, chilling him to the bone. Pulling his cloak tighter around his shoulders, he took in the scenery. Though part of Olympus, the area was free of natural beauty. The familiar sights of birds, fruit trees, and grass were nowhere to be found. The bright light of the sun barely made a dent in the gloom. It was no wonder people wouldn't venture to this desolate part of the realm. The populous of Olympus preferred to ignore the Fates and what they represented, as well as steering clear of the oppressive surroundings.

Eros wasn't so bothered by the roles the women played: Chloe, the most beautiful and youngest of the three, created life; Lacy measured time of existence, while Rose, the oldest and bitterest of the sisters in his opinion, represented death. The woman needed a good romp between the sheets, though he was not volunteering for that duty.

Loud creaking of the door snared his wavering attention. Surprise rocked him to his toes upon seeing Rose's rail thin frame before him, a scowl on her face. He imagined a handmaiden would answer his knock, not the death dealer herself.

Her pale lips curved into a smile. "You showed," she cackled. "I'm impressed." Pulling the door open further, she made a sweeping motion. "Do come in boy. We've been hoping for a bit of fun."

His spine stiffened at her words. "I am no boy, Rose," he rumbled, stepping over the threshold, moving deeper inside.

At the loud slam behind him, he jolted.

"A tad jumpy…boy?" Rose's rusty laugh grated against his ears.

Sucking in a breath, he calmed his nerves. There was no reason to feel apprehensive. He was a God, Son of Aphrodite and Ares. Power flowed through his veins from birth. He brought desire and love to those around him. It should be no different here.

Waiting for Rose to walk ahead of him, he took in his surrounding. The inside of the home was vastly different than outside. He was in some sort of overly large entryway. Bright sun streamed through the top of the cathedral ceiling. Warm tapestries hung on the walls, depicting the various cycles of life. Nude marble statues spanning from the beginning of time dotted the room. Some sexual, some not, but all drew in the viewer.

Rose swept in front of him, the long black dress brushing the floor softly as she walked. Her long black hair swished side to side. A thick grey band of it running along the left side of her face, peeking through every couple of steps. "Come along. I'll take you to Chloe."

Eros grunted and followed as instructed. Shock overrode his nerves when they breached the doorway to another room. It was a veritable sex den. Large, plush, deep red cushions littered the floor. Smaller gold, blue and green pillows defined various areas. His gaze traveled to the right where he found Lacy naked, blonde hair cascading over one shoulder, lounging on her belly. A dark-skinned male consort knelt at her side, rubbing oil over her toned body. She looked up at Eros and grinned. "You did not disappoint, Eros. Bravo. Seems my sister owes me now."

Eros's brows furrowed with confusion. "Chloe didn't think I would show? I find that hard to believe."

"Not her you daft man." She pointed to the woman in front of him. "Her." Rose groaned, earning his attention. The women were becoming more peculiar by the minute. He never would have expected this type of behavior from the women who brought life, longevity, and death to all.

"One night Lacy. You may have your turn with my companion, but I expect Torvald to be well cared for and in pristine condition when he is returned."

"He'll be taken care of, won't he Julian?"

When the man next to Lacy raised his head, arousal glittered in his dark eyes. "Yes, mistress. You have my word."

Rose nodded sharply. "You will find Chloe through those doors, Eros. She vibrated with too much energy to be allowed in here." She pointed to the back of the room at two large blue doors. She stepped to the left to another pillowed seating area. A large, muscular man, wearing nothing but a loincloth, knelt in the middle, his gaze focused solely on Rose. She ran her finger along his shoulders, eliciting a shudder from him. Her gaze snagged Eros's "We are not what you expected, are we?"

"No. Not in the least," he confirmed. They were nothing like what he thought and he had a feeling he had barely scratched the surface.

"Keep that in mind, boy." Moving away from the consort, she slid onto a chaise lounge with all of the grace of a ballerina. "Go now before you see something you may wish you hadn't." The loud snap of her fingers propelled her man in motion. He rose, standing a head taller than Eros's six-foot-six frame. Muscles bulged upon muscles. He was a giant, a Nephilim. When he ambled toward his mistress, Eros took off. There would be many things happening he did not want to see—of that he was sure.

Pushing through the doors, he found the one he was there to see. Chloe stood with her back to the door, staring out a window. She was draped in a fine blue silk shift, her supple body evident underneath. Her long hair brushed the top of her ass, drawing his attention to the perfectly shaped globes.

He may have turned down her invitation to join her in bed, but that didn't mean he wasn't interested. When Zeus commanded your presence, you obeyed. That the summoning had more to do with pleasure than business was a bonus. Now that his task was complete though, he could move on to what would, no doubt, be the best sexual experience he would have to date.

Chloe was a challenge, one he didn't plan on backing away from. She handed him the perfect opportunity to turn his pursuit of her into a much better game when she threw that jealous fit. Little did she know he planned to help her win the bet. If failure were in sight, he would make the match happen without her knowledge. It would be a win-win for them both. Oh, how he enjoyed sparring with her, and with a year of it under their belts, their joining would be explosive.

"I see you made it," she said nonchalantly without turning around.

"You thought I wouldn't?" He moved to stand next to her; surprised to see she was looking out onto a beautiful garden. What madness bewitches this place?

"I meant, made it past my sisters and their men. I didn't doubt you would show up at our home. You love a challenge as much as I do." She turned her head to look up at him. Deep brown eyes gleamed at him. She was aroused, excited by his presence.

He turned away, striding to the side of the room where a plush couch sat against the wall. Easing his body onto it, he did his best to act unaffected by her. "I never have a problem with women. You know that about me. I am the God of love and desire. A flick of my wrist…"

"You mean shot of your arrow…Cupid."

He rolled his eyes at the childish name he had been given eons ago by a jealous Roman unable to pleasure his bride. "As I was saying, a flick of my wrist and I could have all of you begging to make love to me."

Light, bell-like laughter floated through the air. "You are a smug one. You know you hold no power over us."

Eros patted the seat next to him, beckoning her to join him. "Oh but I do, my sweet Chloe. You want me and I'm prepared to let you have me, once you complete your task that is."

Chloe glided toward him, the soft rustle of her clothing the only sound in the room. She chose to stand in front of him, ignoring his invitation. She was a stubborn thing and damn if that didn't turn him on. "Maybe I'm not interested anymore," she said breezily.

Leaning forward, he grabbed her by the waist, pulling her in close. Pressing his nose against the soft triangle of hair covering her pussy, he made a show of breathing in deeply. "You're interested," he breathed out. "You smell like ambrosia; fragrant, rich, and ready to be consumed."

Struggling to get free, Eros let her go. "Get out," she growled.

Chuckling, he leaned back, settling into the cushions. "You accepted the challenge in front of all those people. You can't back out now."

Stomping her foot, she reminded him of a child who didn't get her way. She wasn't used to being told no. He would have to remember that for later. Use the knowledge when they were in bed.

Minutes passed while they stared at each other. The tension in the room rose. Her defiance made his hands itch to toss her over his knee and spank her. To turn her creamy white skin red, make her buttocks burn. She'd enjoy it. He could tell.

A sudden gust of air left her lips. "Let's get this over with."

He sighed. No more fantasies. It was time to get down to business. The quicker they started, the better her chances of success. "I've decided I will give you both of the names to be matched. You'll have to figure out on your own how to get them together."

"Don't do me any favors," she sneered, crossing her arms over her chest.

It was a shame to have her breasts hidden from his view. He would bet the deep red of her areolas matched her lips. He gave his head a quick shake. "I'm not. Having both names will expedite the process and it is no less than I give those who work under me. This case is special though and one I would usually do myself. He is a watcher, Grigori Thane. It's time he earns his wings back."

"A Grigori never loses his wings."

Eros shrugged. "Not in the literal sense."

Tilting her head to the side, she tapped a finger to her lips. Eros was distracted by the move, wondering how they would feel against his again, with her participating, of course. "Hmmm...I remember the name. Slept with one of Zeus's playthings without his permission."

He chuckled. "Yes, that's him. He made the mistake of getting caught. It does not matter now, though. He needs back into the fold."

"Then why not just let him in?"

"It is never that easy. You know as well as I that in order to regain entry into the realm, you must earn your way in. He's to protect an Eternal, Amara Hope."

"That should be simple. He is a watcher after all. Have whomever his keeper is tell him to grab the girl and wait to be transported here."

"Did you forget the reason behind my being here? They must fall in love," he said a bit exasperated. It was as if she didn't want to play the game they'd set up.

Her brow wrinkled and her lips pinched. "I never forget. I merely do not understand why love is a stipulation of his return."

"Zeus will not let him in otherwise."

"Oh? Zeus usually doesn't care."

" He does with this one. When a Grigori falls in love, he cannot be with anyone else from that point forward."

He saw the understanding dawn on her face. Her eyes lit up, dancing with delight. The lips he ached to feel on his flesh, curved into a smile. "It shall be done. I will see you in a month's time. Your place?"

Eros nodded, immediately regretting his compliance. His place would mean they would be alone again. He would not back out though. To do so would put him at a disadvantage. She would know the depth of his need for her then.

CHAPTER ONE

January 3rd

Grigori…Fallen Angel…Watcher…

It didn't matter what people called him. Thane knew the truth. Of all the names in the world, only one described him to a T…Damned.

Damned to hell on Earth fifty years ago because of one simple misunderstanding.

Damned to watch over humans, demons, and other Mystics, while listening for their cries of help. Hoping each time he aided them; it would redeem his image in the eyes of the Gods.

Worst of all, he was damned to obey the whims of a man he once called friend. To bow down before the man; when before they stood on equal ground.

Pushing through the front door of his home at daybreak, the first beams of soft light filtered in behind him chasing the darkness away. The soothing scent of warm leather and cedar washed over his senses, clearing the stench that earlier filled every pore. It felt good to be back home.

"Mark off another lackluster evening watching over the scum of Viral City."

Fuck, he was beat.

Instead of wasting away his days chasing women for sport on Olympus, he now spent each and every waking minute searching for a way to earn his way back into Zeus's good graces. To show his remorse for treading where he shouldn't have. As of yet, he'd had no luck wooing the capricious God.

Shrugging out of his leather jacket, Thane dropped it on a chair just inside his living room, and on his way to the kitchen. His black combat boots squeaked faintly against the dark hardwood flooring. He flipped on the overhead light above the sink, casting the room in a soft, warm glow. It was just enough to light his way.

Immortal or not, his stomach rumbled in protest at the lack of food throughout the night. He prayed Beetah, his new housekeeper, had filled the fridge with his favorite treat: Greek yogurt with lots of honey. It was the closest thing on his earthbound prison that reminded him of the ambrosia he dined on so long ago.

"Don't bother," a deep voice rumbled behind him, as he opened the refrigerator.

Thane immediately closed the door, sucking in a deep breath to mask the emotion that voice invoked before turning around. He leaned back against the stainless steel appliance nonchalantly; feet spread wide, arms crossed over his chest. "Rummaging through my house again, Gabriel?"

The man waved his hand, brushing the intrusion aside as inconsequential. "Only passing the time until you determined your self-imposed penance for the day was fulfilled."

His penance. If anyone looked deep enough, that's what they would see, and that it was true. Self-induced castigation. He wouldn't get into that with Gabriel though. Getting to the bottom of his presence was the first order of business. Then sleep. "Really? And how long have you been waiting this time? Do I need to look for another housekeeper?" Last time Thane found his former friend in the house, the man stayed long enough to eat everything, watch three pay-per-view movies, and lure the ex-housekeeper into bed.

Gabriel chuckled low and steady. "Long enough." A sharp dark eyebrow rose; telling Thane all he needed to know. Looked like a call to the staffing agency would go on his agenda.

"To what do I owe the honor of your visit?"

"Let's move out to the living room. Much more comfortable there." Gabriel rose, towering over the dining table. There was a reason he was one of the Great Watchers: one of four chosen to oversee and guide the Fallen. The man dwarfed Thane by a good five inches, making his own six-foot-six frame seem small in comparison.

He followed his former friend out of the kitchen and into the living room, wondering what brought the man here this time. It was never good news, and he didn't doubt this day's visit would be any different. His presence always set Thane on edge, waiting for the hammer to fall.

Gabriel sank into an overstuffed leather chair, sighing with pleasure. Lips curving up, his eyes slid closed. "You can blame your expensive taste in my staying longer than necessary."

Thane took a seat opposite him on the matching couch. "I'm sure I can blame it on you coming in the first place. You don't visit other Watchers like you visit me. You send them notes when they are tasked."

Gabriel flashed a wide, toothy grin. "Ah, but you are my friend. Would it not be strange if I did not visit you?"

"Were my friend," he muttered, aware Gabriel would hear but not necessarily caring. The man had left him out to dry. Bitterness bubbled in the back of his throat, threatening to choke him.

Gabriel chuckled, seemingly unbothered by the slight. "I could do nothing to get you out of trouble. Dallying with Zeus's consorts can only be done by invitation. The man is possessive with his toys. You knew this. Knew the consequences if you were caught."

Thane grunted, forcing himself to relax back into the supple leather when he felt anything but that. Absently, he stroked the fine grain, allowing the motion to distract his mind. He knew Gabriel was right. He also knew he had been playing with fire; but, damn, it had been good at the time. "As much as I enjoy this walk down memory lane, I've had a long night."

"I'm sure you have. I admit I do not understand your obsession with Viral City. The dwellers there are nothing but vagabonds, addicts, and whores; not fit for the services you insist on providing."

"You wouldn't understand. You still have privileges in the Heavens and on Olympus. You don't know what it's like to be abandoned in this place."

Gabriel made a show of looking around Thane's home, turning his head one way then the other. Scanning over the high-end furniture and expensive fabrics throughout. "From the looks of things, you aren't suffering. You possess all of the funds you need to live a lavish lifestyle. You're free to do as you please when not tasked. You could even have companionship if you wanted."

"Companionship," Thane scoffed at that remark. "You must be joking."

His friend shrugged. "Not all in life revolves around your dick, Thane. I would have thought you would realize that by now."

"Trust me, I have. Not being able to get it up in fifty

years has proven that point exceedingly well. I could never be content to sit and talk with a woman. It would only remind me of what I cannot do, bringing more misery to my life. What use could come of that?"

"You could find a man."

"No," he said harshly. "Never was my thing."

"Either way, it beats what you're doing now. Seething over your exile during the day, while spending your nights with the vilest of creatures. I would pick a beautiful, fresh-smelling man or woman to talk to over that any day."

"That's your opinion. Back to why you're here. I'm sure how I live isn't the reason. Am I to guess I have a new assignment?"

Gabriel studied him with a frankness Thane felt down to his bones. Clenching his teeth, he resisted the urge to squirm under his friend's intense gaze.

Gabriel sighed. "You would be correct. It is a good task too. I'm told if you're successful, you'll be allowed home."

"I am home," he said cheekily. Thane held back the burst of excitement coursing through his blood, refusing to let Gabriel see how the news affected him. He wanted to jump up and shout with joy. Agree to do the task, no questions asked. Say whatever needed to be said in order to leave his earthly prison. To be home, his true home, was a dream he never imagined would come true.

"Don't play me for a fool, Thane. I wasn't born yesterday, and I know this is what you've wanted since the blush of exile wore off. Complete it to their satisfaction, and you'll finally earn your way back into the Heavens and Olympus. You'll be forgiven your transgression, and things will be as if they never happened. You have Zeus's word on it."

Thane looked away. It was almost too good to be true. At the end of the month, it will have been exactly fifty years since he was banished. He wanted to go home.

19

Wanted to be with his family again, with his brothers. He wished for the opportunity with every breath he took. Now, he finally had it within his grasp. He focused on his friend with renewed hope in his heart. "What do I need to do?"

Gabriel grinned. "There is a woman in need of, shall we say, supervision."

Thane's eyebrows shot up. Never before had his assignment been a woman. The rule of the Watchers had always been man for man, woman for woman. It made the tasks less — complicated. "A woman?"

"Yes. It is the ultimate test. We save them until we believe the Fallen is ready."

"And you feel I'm ready." Thane eyed Gabriel warily. The man didn't give off the most confident vibe.

Gabriel leaned forward resting his massive forearms on his knees, seriousness shining in his eyes. "Personally, after watching for so long and seeing no change in your behavior, I question whether you are, but it is not my decision to make. I am doing as I'm told, just as you will do what you are told."

With every fiber in Thane's body, he wanted to jump up and punch Gabriel in the face. Anger filled him at his friend's lack of faith...that his friend thought so little of him.

Instead, he remained seated, face hopefully devoid of emotion. "My behavior is completely changed," he said steadily. "I no longer spend my evenings carousing with women or gorging on so much ambrosia that I don't come out of my stupor for days. I dedicate my free time to those in need. I live a quiet, sedate life."

"But you are still so angry, Thane. You haven't learned what it means to sacrifice for someone else. All of those things you do, you do for you; to make you look better in the eyes of the Gods. Granted, you don't live as luxurious a life as some Watchers. You haven't resorted to drugs to be with women or men. You've kept your body pure for almost fifty years, which is a boon in the eyes of those who've kept watch. What you do not understand though, or have yet to figure out, is what it takes to come home. Believe me, my friend, for I still consider you one, I want you back where you belong."

Thane clenched his jaw to keep his mouth shut during Gabriel's impassioned speech. He knew in the back of his mind that the man tried to help. It didn't though, not now when he was told all of the things he had done over the last couple of decades meant nothing.

They stared intently at each other, a heavy silence filling the room. The grandfather clock stuck six, the repetitive bong echoing throughout the house. He took a deep breath, inhaling the rich leather scent. It calmed him enough to focus on what was important. "What is the woman's name?" Thane finally asked, exhaustion cloaking him, becoming heavier the longer they sat.

"Amara Hope."

Amara. It was a beautiful name. It meant unfading… beloved…eternal. He paused. Eternal…could it be? "She's an Eternal." He didn't pose it as a question. Knew what he was thinking was correct.

Gabriel's mouth curved into a rare, genuine smile; the corners of his eyes crinkled in pleasure. "Very good, Thane. You've gotten it much quicker than anyone else."

He shrugged. "I have a thing for names and meanings."

"Yes, she's an Eternal. Zeus has decided she belongs in his realm."

"Where can I find her?"

"You'll find her in your usual haunt actually, though not as one of the downtrodden. It shouldn't be a problem for you to shift to daytime trolling. Sleep isn't really necessary for you. She's on a bit of a mission of her own. A sort of quest involving someone she loves beyond reason. I wouldn't say she's in danger, but then I wouldn't rule it out being down there."

Thane nodded. She would definitely be in danger in Viral City. No one in their right mind would travel within those four city blocks unless they were looking for trouble. "And an image of her, or am I to figure out what she looks like on my own?"

Gabriel reached inside his long trench coat and pulled out a photograph, sliding it across the coffee table that sat between them.

Thank the heavens for modern technology. Reaching for the picture, Thane picked it up, fumbling it slightly when a small spark shot through his fingertips. Regaining his grip, he looked down and was hit with a bolt of lust. Even fifty-years later, there was no mistaking the feeling.

It appeared to be a candid shot, taken without her knowledge. She stood on a crowed street, a look of desperation etched on her lovely face as she looked over her shoulder. Her deep brown almond-shaped eyes were filled with worry, brows furrowed and full lips compressed. Long dark braided hair ran down her back. Visions of wrapping it around his hand as she kneeled in front of him assailed him instantly. The throb in his groin a shocking yet not unwelcoming result.

Despite being shrouded in concern, he saw the beauty radiating from her. Through the glossy photo she demanded his attention. Begged for his help. Thane had no way to resist. "What exactly must I do?"

"Keep her from doing something stupid."

Thane's head came up in surprise, his gaze clashing with Gabriel's. "As simple as that?"

"It is never as simple as that, but it is all I can say. Final tasks are no walk in the park. You never know what the end result is going to be," he chuckled and stood. "You have her picture and know what is expected. Your task will be complete if she makes it to the end of the month. If, by chance, you figure it all out before then, well, that would be even better."

"Figure it out," he said, but there would be no response. Gabriel had vanished without another word. "Guess I won't be heading to bed." He wouldn't be able to sleep now anyway with his task a priority in his mind.

Snatching up his jacket, he slipped it on as he headed out the front door. His long night just turned into an even longer day.

CHAPTER TWO

January 5th

The woman might actually be the death of him, if that were at all possible. For the third day in a row, Thane followed Amara into the depths of Viral City. Each day she traveled deeper and deeper within. The farther she went, the more dangerous it became, and the more his nerves frayed.

Hunching his shoulders, Thane kept a good distance between him and his quarry. Irritation crawled through him when a drunken man rammed into his shoulder, mumbling incoherently. The smell of alcohol emanating from him so overwhelming, he was sure anyone in a five-foot radius would get drunk off the fumes.

Pushing the man aside, Thane plodded on, keeping Amara in his sight. "Keep her from doing something stupid," he mumbled. "How about pack her in bubble wrap, lock her in a padded room, and throw away the key?" Or tie her to my bed where I can keep her in an orgasmic coma until it is time for her to move on. The thought of her moving on, though, didn't fill him with relief. If anything, his anxiety levels ratcheted up another notch.

It hadn't been difficult to find her the day Gabriel gave him the task. He zeroed in on her the moment she stepped within the border of the four-city block area. The woman stood out like a sore thumb. Slick, dark hair pulled back into a braid, as in the picture. She wore a yellow sweater that hugged her torso like a second skin and her deep blue jeans cupped her legs and ass like a possessive lover. Sturdy boots completed the outfit, and he was oddly thankful for that. There would be no chance of her stumbling and falling to the ground because of spiky, impractical heels. The thing that made her stand out the most was the healthy, vibrant aura around her; it was completely different than the people who actually lived there.

As of yet, no one approached her or tried to snatch her up. She glided through the city as if she were invisible. Hell, being an Eternal, she probably was invisible to many of them.

Eternals had the body of a human, but the soul of an immortal. Zeus, Hades, and Poseidon coveted them. Each trying to snatch them up for their empires…for no other reason than to say they possessed them.

Thane assumed that was why he had been tasked to watch Amara. One of the Gods wanted her. The simple fact that they had to wait until the end of the month before bringing her into the immortal realm could be the reasoning behind his watch. The ambrosia that would turn her immortal would be the sweetest…the most potent then, having fermented throughout the month.

The flash of her bright red jacket snagged his drifting attention, pulling him back to the present.

Her glossy black hair was pulled back into another elegant braid, the tail whipping back and forth with her hurried movements. She cast a glance over her shoulder, forcing him to press up against a dingy brick wall in order

25

to keep well out of sight. Her almond-shaped eyes drifted over him without notice.

As soon as she looked forward again, he shoved away and continued to follow her. Hunting her much like a predator stalked his prey. Each time he saw her, he felt more and more like a beast. More like one of the myriads of shifters roaming the world in human and animal form. Taking what they wanted, when they wanted. Right fucking now, he wanted Amara in his home where he could keep an eye on her without worrying someone would harm her.

Without warning, a woman surged into her, knocking her back a step. Picking up speed, he kept his eye on them, hoping the incident was purely accident. He could see the old crone's mouth move, and her hand clutching Amara's arm to steady herself. The old woman placed a kiss on her cheek, then moved on as if nothing happened. Amara stood rooted to the spot for a couple of seconds before shaking her head and walking again.

Thane released a tension-filled breath he hadn't known he'd been holding and slowed down his pace. Heart beating out of control, he took a second to calm down. That was the most excitement he'd seen in the last three days. If anything more dramatic happened, he didn't think he'd survive it.

Amara shifted directions, hastily skirting a group of men before disappearing from his sight. Anger at her momentary disappearance lit through his body, setting his teeth on edge. Loud, raucous laughter rang out from the men before they broke off, veering into one of the many brothels.

When they disappeared, one thing became apparent. Amara was gone.

Thane sped up, searching the area for any traces of her. His gaze roved over the prostitutes, drug dealers and pimps, as well as the demons masquerading as humans out for a good time.

Glancing down one of the many alleys, he found her thanks to that damn red jacket. She was halfway down the grimy passageway, crouched in front of a large bundle of rags, a man if he wasn't mistaken.

As quietly as possible, Thane made his way toward her, ready to jump in if necessary. As he approached, her soft pleading voice drifted to his ears, doing things to him that it shouldn't. His reaction was more intense than when he first saw her image in the photograph. His cock responded to her soft crooning. Twitching and filling behind the zipper of his jeans with each breathy exhale she made. It was highly inappropriate considering where they were and what his mission was.

"Please Deval, its time to come home. Enough of this foolishness of playing down here. You don't belong in this place." Thane recoiled in disgust as she laid her small hands on the man's arm, seeming not to care about the filth covering him. After all these years, he still couldn't control that reaction.

Overwhelmed with the need to rip her from this other man, Thane fisted his hands next to his sides. It went against the rules to interfere, except when necessary. Threat of dirt, he was sure, didn't count.

The rumpled man grunted while trying to pull away from her. He tipped over, dragging Amara with him.

Thane jumped forward, snatching her up before she landed on the ground. She weighed not more than a feather in his arms. A soft, jasmine scented feather that struggled mightily against him. Her small breasts pressed into his chest and he groaned. His body came alive with a swirl of feelings and emotions. It was an odd reaction, something he noted the day he first saw her picture. The more he saw her, the more his body reacted. The more his body reacted, the more insane with need he became. If this was part of his task, to resist Amara, he had a feeling he would fail miserably. "Calm down, little one," he murmured, stroking a hand down her back. She shivered beneath his touch, rattling his resolve to keep it professional.

All thought of staying on task were blown out of the water when whiskey-colored eyes locked onto his face. There was no fear, only surprise and a flash of something else. It passed too quickly for him to figure out what it was. Her unwavering gaze held him immobile as the seconds ticked by. She was more beautiful than any picture could ever convey.

She licked her full pink lips, drawing his attention. What he wouldn't give to drop a kiss on them. To feel their softness and surrender under his assault his only thought. His yearning must have been stamped across his face.

Renewing her efforts, she pushed against his chest. "Put. Me. Down," she gritted out.

The ball of rags on the ground groaned in pain, breaking the rising tension between them. They shifted their focus. Thane reluctantly let her go but didn't let her get far.

Kneeling on the ground, she pulled the ball of rags up, brushing the hood of his jacket away. "Deval," she whispered, smoothing her hand over his grimy cheek. Thane was oddly jealous at the attention the man received from her. He wanted her hands on him. Stroking his skin. Soothing the fire of arousal threading through his veins.

The man groaned again when she brushed the back of his head. Pulling her hand away, blood coated her fingers.

She gasped, then turned pleading eyes on him. "You have to help me," she implored.

"Do what?" he grumbled. Crossing his arms over his chest, he glared at the other man. Too irritated with his reaction to this woman to care about him. "He put himself in this situation. From the looks and smell of it, he doesn't want out."

"You don't know that," she said heatedly.

"I've been down here enough to know his type." And he had no intention of touching the man. He also wasn't Thane's concern. His job was to protect Amara, not help someone through what would probably be a horrific detox of some sort.

She shot to her feet nimbly, like a cobra striking, meeting him head on. Her tiny, bony finger poked him in the chest. "You don't know his type. You know nothing about him. Where he came from. What he has waiting for him at home. What drove him down here." She looked at Thane with disgust. "I don't know why I even bothered asking a pretty boy like you to help." She rolled her eyes and spun away. Hooking her arms beneath the man's, she tried to haul him to a standing position. She struggled and grunted with exertion but to no avail.

Tipping his head back, Thane stared where the blue skies should be. Smog and filth floated through the air. He would pray for patience to deal with her, but the Gods were never that helpful. "Fuck," he groaned in resolve. Stepping forward he plucked Amara from her spot, setting her to the side. "Let me."

Grabbing the man by the arm, in one smooth move Thane pulled him up, draping the arm over his shoulder and grabbing the man around the waist. The stench rolling off the ball of rags made his eyes water and the urge to vomit crept up his throat. He swallowed down the bile. "What now, little one?" he forced out through gritted teeth.

How she could stand touching or being so close to this man was a feat he didn't think he could accomplish. She needed to make a decision soon as to what the plan of action was or else he would drop the guy back on the ground and toss her over his shoulder. He would take her to his home and hold her captive until the month was over.

Thane focused on the entrance of the alley while he waited. It was a distraction from the man wrapped around him. People shuffled by, attentions elsewhere. The odd few who took more than a passing glance didn't raise any alarms, they only seemed curious about what might be happening.

Amara didn't know what to say. Stunned didn't even begin to cover how she felt. This man, whom she was not afraid of and, in fact, was instantly attracted to, offered to help her with her brother. She wanted to sigh with relief, but knew they needed to leave before someone took more than a passing interest in them.

It was unfortunate she didn't have a plan to extract her brother. Her main goal the past week was to find Deval. She knew she needed to get him home and away from the temptations of Viral City. Start him on the road to recovery, if possible. There was a small part of her that was apprehensive about her ability to find him. His obsession with spending time down there grew each day she was unable to kept him away. It was as if a dark force crawled through him, luring him into the city depths.

"Little one, I need your answer. I can't stand around holding him all day."

The Adonis startled her from her thoughts. A golden aura emanated from him. The color alerting her to his good guy status, at least as she'd been taught by her mother.

He juggled Deval to get a better grip, jostling a groan out.

"Oh! We need to take him home."

Thane's left eyebrow quirked up in silent question.

"To Forest Meadow. Is that okay?"

The Adonis nodded sharply, then started walking. Amara had to practically run to keep up with his long strides.

Damn, his ass looks good in those jeans. The dark denim molded to his ass and thighs, tempting her to reach out and cop a feel.

Horrified at the direction of her thoughts, she didn't pay attention when they emerged from the alley. She got swept up in the sea of people heading in the opposite direction as her brother and the man. Quickly she weaved between the bodies around her and turned back around, catching up to them after a few minutes. They had made it much further than she expected, his long strides eating up the sidewalk. It didn't seem as though the added weight of Deval even mattered to him.

Not wanting to get separated again, she latched onto her brother's other side, intent on holding on. By pure chance, her hand skimmed over the Adonis's arm and she sucked in a sharp breath. The inadvertent touch sent goose bumps along her arm. It was a wholly unexpected sensation, but not unpleasant. The hard-packed muscles of his arm brought fantasies of him wrapping those same arms around her, holding her tight and never letting her go.

"I hope your boyfriend is worth the trouble," he groused, pulling her from her fantasy.

"He's not my boyfriend," she said, not quite sure this was the best place to have a discussion. People were beginning to notice them; sending questioning looks their way.

He grunted in response. "Then why all the trouble?"

She shrugged, knowing he couldn't see it. There were times when she questioned why she did it as well. It always came back to the same thing. "He's my brother," she said finally.

"I'm not sure any of my brothers are worth this stench."

Amara silently agreed. Deval smelled horrible. She would endure though and, if she had to guess, her helper would too. "But you would do it anyway. They're your brothers. Family shouldn't desert family. No matter what happens."

31

"If you say so, lady." At that moment a man bumped into his shoulder, rocking him back on his heels. Even being on the other side of Deval, she felt the underlying tension that passed between the two men in that second of contact. The Adonis wanted to do something about it, but continued moving them forward.

"I'm Amara," she blurted out when she couldn't stand the strain of silence anymore. "Thank you for helping. Not many people would have."

"Thane," he grunted in response. It seemed talking wasn't big on his list of things to do.

They continued to make their way out of Viral City without any other mishaps. The closer they came to the border of town, the cleaner the air got and the worse the stench emanating from Deval. What has he been doing these last few weeks?

Forty minutes later, and after minimal directions, they stood in front of her large, lonely house. The gated entrance the final barrier separating them from their destination. The massive white structure sat back a good fifty feet from the road. Sparse trees and shrubbery making it look cold and uninviting in the light of day.

She looked around the front of Deval at the man who had helped her. "Thanks again for the help, Thane. I've got it from here," she said, hoping he would take the hint. While she may not be afraid of him, she had enough presence of mind to know she shouldn't let him in the house.

"You don't want me to carry him inside? That's quite a distance from here to the front door." A golden eyebrow rose, a little grin kicking up the corner of his mouth. Her silly heart fluttered in her chest at the sexy smirk painted on his face. They both knew she would need the help.

Looking at the distance between the gate and the front door again, she figured she could manage that—barely. Then she thought about having to carry Deval upstairs… that she couldn't do. He was at least a hundred pounds heavier than her — dirty rags and all.

"Um," she licked her lips nervously. Could she let him inside? Would she be safe with him? Yes, her inner voice yelled.

"I promise, I'm not here to hurt you. Like you pointed out, I'm only trying to help out."

Amara looked at the house again. It would be nice to have some assistance for once. To be able to count on someone when she needed them most.

"I'll let you in, but I reserve the right to call the police."

He nodded and his grin grew wider. "Of course."

CHAPTER THREE

January 5th – Afternoon

Thane wondered if Amara would mind if he stripped down and jumped in the shower she had running. His clothes were ruined. He smelled funky. Even after a night of watching over the city, he never smelled this bad. Worst of all, all of that hot, relaxing water was wasted while waiting for a man to come out of his stupor enough to undress.

When Thane and Amara made it into the house, she immediately maneuvered them upstairs to what she explained was her brother's bathroom. Through her nervous rambling, Thane learned the home was left to the siblings when their parents passed away a couple years ago. Amara took over the master bedroom and the bulk of the upkeep, while Deval stuck to the second floor, doing the least amount of work possible. The arrangement worked for them; though Thane got the impression she would gladly welcome help from her brother.

Stepping into the upstairs bathroom, he lowered Deval to a padded bench situated against a wall. Amara scurried around the bathroom getting everything ready while Thane stood watch. Her brother was groggy and near unresponsive. The head wound the likely source, and medical attention might be needed.

That brought a slew of questions rushing to his mind. Just because Amara was an Eternal, did that make her brother one as well? Did an Eternal actually need to see a doctor? Being human, they may need one. Humans certainly didn't come with tough outer shells. He sure as hell didn't know about Eternals though, and would be asking her later...once they got Deval settled.

During the trek to her place, he decided he would tell her upfront why he was there. It would be easier to protect her, keep her out of trouble, if she knew. Maybe that would curb her risky behavior and make the next couple of weeks breeze by without incident.

Leaning against the bathroom doorframe, he watched as the tiny woman wrestled with her brother. So much trouble for one so undeserving. Gabriel might have been right about Thane's actions, now that he thought about it. He should have just bided his time with other pursuits when he wasn't tasked.

Amara attempted to wake Deval up again, with little success. The man moaned and groaned. Unintelligible whispered words trickled out of his mouth. Thane knew he should go lend a hand, but he was over the Good Samaritan shtick. Shifting positions, a fresh wave of stench rolled off him. He looked down at his clothes.

Fuck, my favorite jacket. Thane groaned and pulled the jacket off. Neither Amara nor her brother noticed his anguish. He contemplated the jacket in his hands, manipulating it to see if there was any actual damage to it. Maybe he could drop it by the cleaners and see what they could do. There had to be ways to get the smell out without ruining it. Wouldn't hurt to see.

Sighing in disgust, his attention was drawn back to the siblings.

Rag after dirty rag was peeled away from Deval's body and thrown into a pile at his feet. They would need to be burned. No amount of washing would get them clean again. Idly, he wondered if his own would need to join the pile. He sniffed his shirt, lost in his own drama. No, they'll come clean. They aren't that bad. On the heels of that thought, he remembered something important. Shit, I need a new housekeeper. It took him a second to realize Amara stood in front of him.

She snapped her fingers in front of his face. "Hey, Thane." Her brows dipped and forehead creased. He felt the urge to caress her face and smooth away the worry. "Can you help me get him up? I need to get his pants off."

He shook his head, bringing him out of his daze. Thane's gaze went from her angelic, pleading, heart-shaped face to that of her brother's. The man mumbled incoherently but didn't move. His features were scrunched like something bothered him. The guy was dead weight.

Dropping his jacket on the floor, he crossed to where the guy was slumped against the wall. There would be no easy way to do it. Squatting down, he slipped his hands under Deval's arms and pulled him up. He tried to keep their bodies from touching, leaving space for Amara to undress him, but when the back of her hand skated across the front of his jeans, he knew it hadn't been enough space. Surprisingly, his cock reacted—jerking—coming to life, again, behind the tight denim. His gaze landed on her face to see if she even realized it.

She had. Her eyes rounded, mouth opening on an exaggerated O. She was as surprised as he was by his response. No doubt, but for two entirely different reasons.

"Oh," she squeaked out. "Um, I'm sorry about that." The prettiest blush painted her cheeks, turning her light brown skin a deep red.

Thane didn't know what pleased him more; the fact his body had a sexual reaction or that she noticed. It had been almost fifty years since he'd felt desire, since his brain and cock were in sync, and the end result was purely physical. It was a heady feeling to have it happen, and he didn't quite know what to do with it. Shouting for joy and tackling her to the ground; two options he didn't think she would appreciate.

Amara stepped back and stammered. "I'm so sorry. I didn't mean." Her words trailed off as she gestured to his crotch.

Thane couldn't stop the chuckle from coming out. Part amused, part aroused, he was one hundred percent ecstatic his body was alive in the first place. "Don't worry about it. Get him undressed and we'll get him cleaned up. Then maybe later we can talk about...that."

Amara swallowed hard. She really didn't mean to brush her hand over his pants. They were just there when she reached around Deval. Her gaze traveled over Thane, stopping when she reached...the spot. The fabric stretched tight across his hips. The bulge behind the zipper growing larger the longer she stood there staring...like a girl who'd never seen an erection before. Arousal flooded her, and her core clenched at the thought of being filled by him.

Yeah, we'll talk about it later.

He cleared his throat, drawing her attention back to his amused face. She felt her own heat even more. She didn't know if they should talk about it or just act on it.

Act on it. Definitely.

Quickly, she glanced down his body again. He was fucking hot and had a body she wouldn't mind exploring. Deval was back safely in the house, and she could use the stress relief. Thane looked more than willing to roll around on the bed with her. Or pin her up against the wall. Bend her over the kitchen table and rail her from behind. Any of those positions, or all of them, would do. Fast, hard, rough fucking was definitely called for after weeks of worry.

A shiver wracked her frame. With more care than she had taken before, she slipped her hand between the men and unbuttoned Deval's pants. Getting behind him, she reached around his waist, grasped the band, and pulled them down, leaving his grungy boxers in place.

"Those too," Thane grunted. "Won't do any good to clean him up if he's still wearing something so disgusting."

Amara turned her face away, not wanting to see what was revealed. There were some things a sister should not be subjected to. A brother's naked ass was definitely one of them.

How she ever thought she would be able to do this on her own, she had no idea.

Thane dragged her brother to the shower, waiting for her to open the long glass door. Once it was open, heat enveloped them as he stepped inside, walking directly under the hot spray. The white T-shirt Thane wore was quickly soaked and molded to his chest. Water ran down his arms, trickling over thick defined muscles. Her breath caught in her throat. Even with her brother plastered to him, Thane was a thing of beauty. He deserved time to be appreciated.

"I'm going to need a little help in here," he rumbled out, his piercing green eyes locked onto her face. There was hunger in his face, and it was directed right at her. She would lie to herself and say she didn't know what it meant.

Heat of a completely different kind flooded her body and sent her pulse racing, but the words set her in motion. Amara shimmied out of her jeans and stripped her shirt off, leaving on her bra and panties. It would be easier to move around under the water. Everyone knew wet denim was a nightmare. She looked down at herself and hoped the intimate items didn't become transparent in the water. If they did, well it wouldn't matter. Her priority was getting Deval cleaned up and put into bed. She would deal with the embarrassment later.

Grabbing a puff and a bottle of body wash, she stepped in with the men. Thank goodness the bathroom had one of those multi-person corner glass shower stalls. The three of them would fit in there with plenty of room to maneuver. There was even a small stone seat to sit Deval on when it got too much for Thane. Not that she thought it would ever get to that point. She got the impression nothing wore him out.

Setting that delicious thought aside, Amara set about scrubbing her brother with single-minded ferocity, while refusing to look at Thane unless absolutely necessary. The heat in the shower was barely bearable, but she wasn't sure the temperature of the water was the problem. The one time their gazes locked, desire coursed through his. His eyes narrowed, smoldering and darkening the longer she stared. It was a sheer act of will to pull away and get back on task.

Working together, they were able to get Deval as clean as he would get at the moment. She gently scrubbed his hair, aware of the wound on the back of his head. Once all of the blood was washed away, she found a medium-sized gash that had already started to heal. Her brother moaned every once in a while and even tried to push her away.

At least he's responding some.

Stepping out, she grabbed a towel, wrapping it around her body, and snatched up a few more for the guys. Walking back into the humid space, she handed a towel to Thane, who looked at her with lust in his deep green eyes. It hit her, once again, how intimate the setting was. Well, aside from her brother's presence. He kind of put a damper on the whole thing.

Later. We'll have time later.

"Prop him up on the seat. I'll get him while you dry off," she said, her voice steadier than she imagined it would be. As she tended to her brother, the sound of drenched fabric hitting the floor reached her ears. She was powerless to keep from gawking at Thane. Her Adonis had pulled his shirt off and worked on the button of his jeans. Her gaze bounced from his trim waist, over his six-pack abs and smooth golden chest up to his face. The slow curl of his lips, along with the naughty intentions gleaming from his eyes, was almost too much to resist.

She wanted to crawl over to him, brush his hands from the top of his jeans, and be the one to reveal the rest of his body. It was highly inappropriate behavior to have about a man she had just met. But then, she wasn't a saint and he had a body worth sinning for.

Sucking in a harsh breath, she forced her attention back to Deval. When Thane took the few steps over to where she knelt, she couldn't help but notice the towel she had handed him hung precariously from his hips. With one light tug, she would get an up close and personal view of his entire body. A view she desired to see with every fiber of her being. She licked her lips at the thought of tasting his skin. A body like his deserved every bit of her attention. Hands. Lips. Teeth. There would be no inch left undiscovered by her—if she had the chance. Any other time and she would be all over the man.

"What now, little one?" His voice flowed over her like molasses, smooth, rich, and dark. A shiver raced down her spine, but she forced her attention back to her brother.

She cleared the arousal forming in her throat. "Bed. Need to get in bed."

A low growl came from Thane. "That can be arranged."

She felt her cheeks grow hot. "Deval, I mean. Need to get him in bed."

Thane grunted then pulled her brother up. Amara wrapped a towel around his waist a second before he was hoisted in the air.

She followed Thane out, then rushed around him to turn the bed down. With a bounce and a groan from Deval, he landed on the clean sheets. Tossing the covers over him, Amara tucked him in and stepped back. There was nothing else she could do for him at the moment.

Wonder if he wants to play. Unerringly, her gaze landed on the man crowding her thoughts. Arms crossed over his broad chest. Droplets of water dripped from his hair, chasing each other down his sculpted body. His eyes crinkled at the corners as he smiled.

Would it be too forward to grab his hand and lead him straight to her bed? She could thank him for all of his help in the most primal and pleasurable way possible.

CHAPTER FOUR

January 5th – Afternoon

Thane studied the woman standing on the other side of the bed as she tucked her brother in. An air of self-sacrifice whirled around her. Caring and concerned, she poured all of her energy into her brother, not once thinking of herself; or the fact that she was in harm's way.

He didn't know if he should throttle her for her actions; or allow the feeling of pride he felt for her to spread through him.

One thing was for certain, now that he'd found a way to be next to her, he intended to stay.

Helping her with her brother can't be the task. Gabriel said to keep her out of trouble. Could the brother be it?

He studied the sleeping form on the bed. The man would be too weak to do anything at the moment. The most action the guy would see was sleep and, at some point, food. He was the perfect picture of unhealthy. What would happen when he regained his strength? A bit on the thin side, a few hearty meals would bring him back to life.

Could whatever lured him to Viral City come back? Was that the reason Thane was here?

Amara sighed and walked out of the room, heading back into the bathroom. He followed suit, unable to resist doing otherwise. She leaned over in the shower to pick up the clothes he'd dropped. "I'm going to wash our things. I hope you don't mind."

"Not at all. I wasn't looking forward to getting back into them." It also meant he had more time with her.

She chuckled and gathered her clothes. He wished like hell she hadn't wrapped up in that damn towel. He wasn't oblivious to her stripping before stepping into the shower with them. The only things holding him back from pinning her against the wall were the wet jeans he wore and the man he'd held in his arms.

Her satiny pink panties and matching pink lace bra set off her light brown skin. Gorgeous breasts, curvy waist and thighs, she was the ideal of feminine beauty. He wanted to sip the water cascading over her body, knowing it would taste of her. When the lace of her bra became drenched and her deep red nipples puckered, he'd wanted to drop Deval to the ground and concentrate on her. Her body called to him and he damn sure wanted to answer.

Fuck, even now that she was covered up, just seeing her bare neck and the curves of her shoulders got him hard. The towel around his waist wouldn't hide his painful erection.

She walked over to the pile of rags she'd peeled from her brother, and he stopped her with a hand on the shoulder. The smooth skin beneath his hand was soft and warm. Pinpricks of sensation ran through his arm, stabbing him in the chest. He rubbed his free hand over his heart trying to ease the pain away. *Damn, what is she doing to me?*

He couldn't voice his thoughts at the moment. Doubted she would have an answer. "Leave them. They need to be burned."

43

She gulped and nodded. He could see the want in her eyes, but she held back. He was strangely happy that she did. The emotions boiling to the surface within him were throwing him off. He needed a couple moments to figure out how to handle it all.

Fifty damn years and nothing aroused him, neither man nor woman. Not skilled courtesans or eager young lovers. All it took was one look at this tiny woman and firecrackers lit off like the Fourth of July. Desire for her built up like steam in a kettle ready to blow its top. His skin felt sensitive to the touch. His sight brighter and clearer. It was a lot to wrap his head around. He had gotten used to feeling nothing. Counted on it when helping others. He usually kept a distance, something he found he struggled with around Amara.

Sure, he acted put out and irritated. As if the entire situation bothered him. It did, but not on the level people would imagine. He was exhilarated and intrigued by what happened inside him and yet afraid of what it meant. This had to be a test.

Thane snapped out of his musings when he heard the door click shut. Glancing into the bedroom, he saw Deval lying still and unmoving beneath the covers. Leaving the room, he made his way downstairs. Noise from the kitchen pulled him in that direction.

Amara rummaged in the pantry, still clad in her towel. Sounds of the washing machine running filled the air. On the stove, he saw a pot waiting for whatever she planned on making. How long had he stood there lost in a daze?

"Anything I can do to help?" he asked, aware he had startled her when she gasped and spun around. The sound did nothing to assuage the arousal in him.

Letting out a breath, she turned back to her task. "No. I'm going to make some soup. Something that will be easy to get down Deval's throat. I've never seen my brother look so skinny and pale."

Thane wanted to comment on what he thought the

issue was, but the memory of her bony finger stabbing him in the chest stopped him.

Leaning in the doorway, arms crossed over his bare chest, he tilted his head to the side to watch her in action. She moved with quiet grace, gliding back and forth throughout the kitchen: the pantry...the fridge...the stove. Her hips, covered by the terry cloth, swished from side to side tempting him. Pure beauty in motion.

Minutes went by without a word. The comfort Thane felt ended abruptly when a sharp crackle disturbed the air around him, and the temperature dropped suddenly. His spine snapped straight as he pushed away from the doorframe.

"I'll be right back," he mumbled, not waiting for a response. A dark presence had entered the house. He felt it in his bones, grating over his heightened senses.

Quickly, he made his way through the lower level, all the while hyper aware of his surroundings. Mounting the stairs he quietly made his way to the upstairs bedroom Deval resided in, knowing he was the cause of the chill and oppression creeping through the home. He felt at a slight disadvantage traipsing around in only a towel. Good thing he wasn't bashful.

Edging his way into the room, he found Deval was no longer alone. A petite young woman with long black hair stood next to the bed. Her bright red lips were pulled down into a frown. Her brow furrowed. "He isn't much to look at," she said thoughtfully. Reaching out, she ran a finger down his face. Deval moaned low, turning toward her, his eyes never opening. "I hoped for a better reward. Maybe by the time he is to become mine, he will have improved."

"Why would he go with you at all?" Thane asked.

The woman didn't startle at his sudden presence. "He is promised to me," she stated as a matter of fact. She looked up at him with glowing red eyes. "He will go because it is his fate. Because he will want no one else."

45

Demon. Thane shouldn't be surprised. Demons were inherently attracted to scum. Unfortunately, Amara risked her life to save this particular one, and Thane would do anything to prevent him from being taken. He knew it would hurt Amara terribly if that happened. "You're right, he isn't worth much. If you say he's your reward, then you should ask for something better."

The demon looked down at Deval. She brushed a lock of dark hair from his brow in a loving manner. He moaned and shifted closer, as if seeking her touch. "No. He has many months to improve. I will keep him. Besides, I have been loyal to Hades since my inception and brought up by the hand of the woman he loves. To reject their gift would be a slight to them both." She glanced toward Thane again. "You must be the keeper of the other."

"The other?" His thoughts immediately went to Amara. The demon could mean no one else.

Her head tilted to the side as she studied him. "They're twins. Yin and Yang. As we," she motioned between them with her hand, "are opposites, so are they. Did your handler tell you nothing?"

Thane firmed his lips, holding his tongue. Of course Gabriel told him nothing. Over the years he had grown used to the lack of information. Always figuring things out as he went. This time though, there seemed more to the task. In the back of his mind, Thane knew this but refused to focus on it at the time. Now he was caught off guard and ill informed. A demon knew more about what his task was than he did. It was a bitter pill to swallow.

"I can see from your expression, he didn't tell you shit. This must be your last task. Am I correct, Grigori? Are you to be forgiven your transgressions and placed back into the Heavens or on Olympus?"

Thane grunted in answer. She could take what she wanted from it.

The demon laughed. "The Gods are funny beings, I'll give you that. Forever thinking they are better than everyone else. Always playing their minions for the fool. At least Hades allows us to know what the end game is. No surprises where he's concerned, and it keeps demons and tortured souls in their place. My advice to you, you'd do well to think beyond your needs and gain."

That was the second time in less than a week he was reminded of that. It was a notion he needed to think more about. But he wanted to know what she knew. How she came to such an idea. "Why would you say that?"

"That's how it always is with your final mission," she said rolling her eyes. "Nothing is ever as it seems. There is meaning in all of it, and usually the answer is right in front of your face. Or in your case — downstairs. I've been around long enough to see a good number of Grigori earn their wings back."

Irritation ran down Thane's spine. Releasing his hold on his limited powers, he allowed his wings to manifest. The slight tingling on his back, turning into a fiery burn as large white-feathered wings appeared. It was a juvenile show, but damn he was tired of people assuming he'd actually lost them. He flexed the wings, allowing them to stretch out, nearly touching the walls of the room. The whisper of the feathers brushing together, a light draft of air the result. "Still got 'em."

"Good for you," she said sarcastically, clearly unimpressed. "I bet you think you have a big dick too."

Seconds later, his wings folded in and disappeared. "What are you doing here, demon?"

"Falcon. My name is Falcon. I only came to check on what's mine. I looked for him in the city and didn't find him. Figured the other one brought him home."

"Now that you've seen him and know he is being cared for, you can leave. He won't be going with you any time soon." Thane walked to the other side of the bed, planting his feet wide and crossing his arms over his chest. He eyed the man in the bed, then glared at Falcon. It didn't matter what look Thane had on his face, any attempts at intimidation wouldn't work with the woman. She wasn't even paying attention to him.

With frank curiosity, she studied Deval. A look of concern flickered in her eyes. Without looking up, she addressed him. "I will have your name before I leave. I would like to know who to thank."

Maybe it was the fledgling affection or possessiveness she showed, whatever it had been, he told her what she wanted to hear. "Thane."

"And the other?" She jerked her head to indicate Deval. "His twin?"

"Amara. And she's mine. Under my protection," he growled.

Falcon chuckled lightly. "More than you realize, Grigori. Thank you," she murmured seconds before disappearing.

Thane didn't have time to contemplate Falcon's words. Amara appeared in the doorway with a tray full of food.

"Is everything okay?" She stepped into the room warily. Small measured steps as she looked around the room.

"Its fine, little one." He took the tray from her, allowing her to sit on the bed.

"We need to wake him to get him to eat. We can prop him up on the pillows to make it a little easier."

Thane set the tray of food down on the empty nightstand. Rounding the bed, he jerked Deval to a sitting position, waiting until Amara stacked the pillows behind him before leaning him back.

She cupped Deval's face, crooning at him. "Deval, sweetie, its time to wake up. You need to eat."

Deval groaned. His eyes fluttered but remained closed.

"Deval, you have to wake up," she said, softly brushing the hair back from his head. Thane was certain the soft and gentle technique wouldn't work. The man needed a rude awakening. Slapping his face would be frowned upon. Amara didn't look like the type to let something like that pass without words or retribution.

Walking to the windows, he threw open the curtains. The last rays of sunlight streamed in, brightening the dark room. Lifting the window, a burst of cold air came sweeping in, rushing through the room, and dropping the temperature even more than when the demon was there.

Heading back to the bed, Thane whipped back the covers, exposing Deval's towel-clad body. Goose bumps rose on the man's skin as the wind brushed over him. His eyes fluttered more, cracking open a bit.

"Thane," Amara screeched. She went to grab the covers, but he stopped her.

"It'll wake him up better than what you were doing. He's too far under for soft cooing."

"No he isn't…"

"Amara?" Deval croaked.

She rushed back to his side, pulling the sheet up. She offered him a sip of water, which he took greedily. "Deval, I was so worried."

"Where am I?" The man looked around the room, confusion weighing his eyebrows down.

"Home. I found you in Viral City."

Deval's eyes popped open wide. "No," he gasped.

"Yes." She grabbed his hand, stroking the back of it.

Thane saw the tears gather in the corner of her eyes. The sight screwed with the need to keep it professional. How professional was it to keep imagining her on her knees in the shower blowing you?

49

"I…" She sputtered to a stop.

"I'm sorry, Amara," Deval said. Thane watched as the energy drained from him.

Leaning forward, she dropped a kiss on Deval's forehead. "You're home now, sweetie." She looked at Thane and smiled, then turned her attention back to her brother. "We'll help you through it, but first you need some food."

Thane felt the weight of Deval's regard. Their gazes clashed. Deval's one of question and gratitude. Thane… well, he didn't know what the man saw. All he knew was what he felt simmering inside. Jealousy at the peck on the head, and the attention the man got from his sister. Even knowing Amara acted out of love didn't help stem the tide of envy. Fast on the heels of that foreign feeling, a sense of longing snaked through him. The unwelcome feelings made him scowl.

A driving need to leave the room, and the affection swarming around him propelled him across the room to the door.

"I'm going to check on the clothes." Turning on heel, he left the room. He needed to get a hold on the whirlwind of emotions, and that wouldn't happen standing in a room with the brother and sister.

CHAPTER FIVE

January 5th – Late afternoon

Amara left Deval asleep in his bed. Exhaustion pulled him under a couple of minutes after Thane left the room. He said no more about what happened to him or why he had been in Viral City.

The week he had been missing felt like the longest of her life. For countless hours on end she searched for him. Popping down to his favorite hangouts to see if any of his friends knew where he could be. She caught a break when one of them told her she overheard him talking about Viral City. That was what had her combing the streets there for the last few days.

Now that she'd found him, she could finally take a breath. Finally take a moment to not think or worry about him. He wouldn't be able to go anywhere in his current condition. Unfortunately, that couldn't be said about the man that helped her rescue him.

"Thane," she breathed lightly as she walked downstairs. His name rolled off her tongue as if she always said it. It sent warmth through her that she hadn't

51

felt in years. Not since her parents died and left her in charge of everything. The house. The bills. Her brother.

Even knowing Thane the short amount of time she did, she knew he was an enigma. The disgusted looks he leveled at Deval irritated her, but then he turned around and helped pick him up and carry him home without complaint. He assisted her in getting him cleaned up, and when she went into the bathroom to grab the pile of filthy clothes, they were gone.

He helped even though he acted annoyed. At the moment, with Deval cleaned, fed, and resting, she knew he prowled downstairs waiting for her — well, she hoped. A thrill at the thought skittered through her body. She wouldn't mind being the focus of his attention for a couple hours, possibly longer. Maybe he would be up to helping her relieve the stress after the week she'd had. From the looks he shot her way, she didn't think he would mind.

Emerging on the first floor, she went into the kitchen to look for him. His mention of checking on the laundry flickered through her mind. She doubted he knew how to even operate the machine. He looked to be the kind of guy who had someone do it for him.

Like a girlfriend.

Amara brushed the thought aside. If he had a woman waiting for him somewhere, she didn't think he would be in Viral City assisting random strangers. Nor did she think he would stay around to help her out. A Good Samaritan only went so far.

Stepping into the laundry room she didn't find Thane, but she did see the dryer running. The clothes were softly thumping around.

Guess I was wrong about that.

Retracing her steps, she went through the kitchen and into the living room. The faint sound of water running grabbed her attention, pulling her through the office library and toward her bedroom. The closer she got, the

52

louder the sound, and the more the thoughts of running her hands over his naked body flashed through her head.

Amara froze in the open doorway of her bathroom at the sight before her. Steam poured over the top of the glass shower wall and, through the mist, was the hazy form of Thane naked as naked could get. He faced away from her; head thrust under the spray, so she didn't think he'd heard her arrival. Droplets of water ran down the glass enclosure revealing small lickable tidbits of his skin. From what she could see, her imagination paled in comparison to what he really looked like sans clothes.

The driving need to join him echoed in her brain. Her nipples stood at attention, as warmth crawled through her, ending in her belly. A fire lit her up from the inside, burning brighter with lust as the seconds ticked by.

Why was she so drawn to the man? What was it about him that made her want to be with him?

The 'why' didn't actually matter, at least not at the moment. She wanted him and she would have him.

Before she could think better of it, she dropped her towel, took off her bra and panties, and strode across the room. Opening the glass door, she was assaulted by steam and hot water mixed with the earthy scent of man.

Thane didn't move from where he stood. He continued to let the water beat down over his body, oblivious to her drinking him in. He was a vision of tan, muscular skin from head to toe. The ass she'd checked out earlier was as firm as she thought it would be. His waist was tapered and perfect for wrapping her legs around. The strength that ran through him was undeniable.

While soaking him in, he turned around, stepping out from under the spray. His hand was wrapped around his hard cock, stroking leisurely. "I wondered if you would actually join me."

Her only answer was to hum as her gaze bounced from his face to his hand then back up. His eyes darkened with lust, nostrils flared. Licking her lips, the earlier memory of the previous shower flashed in front of her. Bare chest, hands on his pants ready to reveal the treasure hidden beneath.

She wanted to feel his dick pulse in her mouth. Taste him and learn what made him moan and lose control. Stepping toward him, she stopped in front of him and dropped to her knees. Brushing his hand away, she gripped his shaft. Thick and long, it would be a chore to take it all in. To let it touch the back of her throat without gagging before swallowing the head. Damn, she couldn't wait to try though.

She teased him with long, slow strokes. Her fingers barely meeting as they glided up and down his shaft. He grunted and tried thrusting faster, making it his pace and not her own. Placing a hand on his hip, she skimmed up his chest over rock hard abs to distract him. Lightly raking her nails on the trip back down before she cupped his balls and tugged. He stopped pushing his hips forward and let her set the pace.

For too long she'd neglected her sexual needs. Her last boyfriend leaving soon after her parents died, and her life became consumed with picking up the pieces. A casual hook up here or there kept her desires at bay, satisfied but not really satisfied.

She loved sex. Sucking cock. Being eaten out by a man who knew what a clit was and how to use it to give a woman's unimaginable pleasure. Masturbating. Fucking. Playing.

She didn't hold to the belief that a woman couldn't take what she wanted. That she shouldn't enjoy sex. It was archaic and idiotic thinking in her opinion. Sex should be fun and playful or hard and demanding or whatever the hell you wanted it to be, as long as everyone involved consented and enjoyed it.

Her pussy tingled and her stomach fluttered with need. Unable to resist any longer, she stuck her tongue out and swirled it around the tip of his penis before closing her lips around it. The soft skin, velvety smooth but laced with steel beneath her lips. A long hiss escaped Thane when she dipped her tongue into the slit seeking out the salty, sweet confection only he could produce.

Laving the head as she worked her hand up and down his shaft, squeezing just a little bit harder as she brought it closer to her mouth. Pre-come leaked onto her tongue, making her moan. He tasted so fucking good. Masculine — clean — musky. Gradually she worked her mouth down. Gobbling up more of him with each pass.

"Amara," he groaned. His hand landed on her head, and she wished her hair were down. What she wouldn't give to have him wrapping his fists in it, forcing her deeper onto him. She barely noticed when his hand slipped over the back of her scalp to pick up her braid. He pulled hard, catching her off guard. On her gasp, he thrust deeper, not stopping until he was all the way in.

Pulling in deep breaths through her nose, she willed herself to relax and allow him to use her like he wanted. Bumping the back of her throat, she swallowed quickly, thrilled when she heard a gruff moan from him.

Her pussy demanded action, but from the sounds Thane made, she didn't think he would last long enough to ram his dick in her. Keeping one hand wrapped around his cock, she sought out her clit with the other. Her fingers slid over her nearly naked pussy lips, which were coated with arousal. Using her middle finger, she pushed through her swollen flesh, circling her pulsing nub with increasing insistence. She needed to come...and quick. Then she could concentrate on getting Thane to shoot his seed all over her.

In no time, tingles started down in her toes and worked their way up her legs. Her pussy quivered, her nipples hardened. Dropping her hand from him, she thrust two fingers into her pussy, pumping fast and furious as the pressure built. She quit moving on his shaft, sucking in as much as possible, and holding him in her mouth as she moaned out in orgasmic ecstasy. She shuddered and jerked, getting sucked into her own world of dancing lights and muted sounds. There was something about coming while still sucking your partner's dick that made the release that much better.

As soon as she regained her senses, she felt the weight of Thane's regard. Only a thin green ring was left around his blown pupils. His nostrils flared and his breathing labored. With a slightly shaky hand, she gripped him again, attacking him with renewed force. She fondled his balls and felt them draw up, signaling his impending release. Sucking him deep, she worked him over with her lips, tongue, teeth, and hand. Not slowing down until she pulled his orgasm from him. A strangled cry from above and she popped off him, jacking him off onto her chest.

Thane stumbled back against the wall, eyes closed, chest heaving. Amara got to her feet, locking her wobbly legs and stepped under the spray of the water. With efficient moves, she washed her body, leaving her hair in the braid. She would need to take it down sooner or later, but didn't feel like messing with it at the moment.

A quick glance at Thane, and she saw he still struggled to catch his breath. She opened her mouth to ask if he was all right, but he held up his hand, stopping her.

"I'm fine. Just need a minute. It's—been awhile."

Surprise had her snorting in disbelief, but she decided not to say anything. Turning off the shower, she left him leaning against the wall. As much as she enjoyed the moment, she wasn't about to start coddling someone else. The whole interlude with Thane was purely stress relief.

Thane emerged from the bathroom and strode across Amara's bedroom like he owned the place. Hell, he felt like the king of the world after what just happened. His period of abstinence was over thanks to the little vixen in disguise. Her unashamed desire rocked him and all thoughts of her being a sweet, naïve creature were

56

obliterated. She had dropped to her knees and taken what she wanted from him without glancing back when she was done.

He thought he could keep the woman off his mind while showering. He had been so very wrong. Deciding to use her bathroom had been his biggest mistake. The second he turned on the water and the room filled with her soft jasmine scent, he figured out the flaw in his plan. His shaft came to life and his skin became ultra sensitive. All thoughts of avoiding her and keeping his distance evaporated with his common sense.

He didn't know how long he stood under the water waiting for her. Hoping she would come find him. It sounded so desperate to him now. Not once in his life had he longed for a woman to make the first move. It proved how out of practice he was after all.

Standing under the hot spray, he was seconds from getting out when she finally joined him. The lust and need sparkling in her eyes, and the way she devoured him with her gaze, told him he was in for a ride. He didn't count on her going to her knees and blowing him. Honestly, he had no idea what would happen.

For the love of Zeus, it had been the best blowjob he'd had in centuries. He remembered what sex felt like: the rush of endorphins, slick skin sliding against slick skin, the heated clasp of his lover's body, and finally, the euphoric feeling of climax. It came as a punishment, a reminder of what he had done wrong.

But those memories didn't live up to Amara and how she made him feel. There was a connection he had never known, a link binding them together that had nothing to do with his task.

The touch of her hand on his skin made him ache for more. The lust in her eyes made him want to cover her, fill her, and watch her explode. The twinge in his heart, which tended not to be involved, told him he needed to tread carefully. Maybe it was finally getting a response from his long-dormant body. Perhaps it was helping someone truly in need. It might even be that he thought he could actually fall in love. He didn't know the reasons, but it scared the shit out of him...if he thought about it too long.

White towel wrapped around his hips, he stopped next to the bed where she had laid out his clothes. The clean shirt and fresh denim ready to be put on. "Ready to have me leave so soon?"

She shrugged and stepped into a pair of black yoga pants. She shimmied them up her hips seductively before sliding a dark pink tank top over her head, covering her naked breasts. "That's entirely up to you. I appreciate all of the help, but if you need to go, then go."

Gathering up her wet towel she brushed by him, snagging his as she went. It came off with little effort. His cock started to fill as the cool air in the room drifted over him. It was like the thing had a mind of its own now.

Grumbling, he pulled on his jeans and left his T-shirt where it lay. He didn't plan on leaving. In fact, he hoped to stay the night.

He leaned against the door to her bathroom and watched her putter around. She dropped the towels in a hamper, then busied herself in front of the mirror. It felt so damn domestic, it should have been sickening, but it didn't feel that way.

She took her time running another towel along her braid, wringing the water out, and then put moisturizer on her face. She looked at herself in the mirror and nodded in satisfaction. Quick, simple and he liked it.

He saw her sneak a glance at him in the mirror, the corners of her lips curving into a smile. "I take it you're staying?"

Thane nodded and followed her out of the bathroom. Heading through the library, she swerved right to head up the stairs. "I'm just going to check on Deval real quick, then we can talk. I'll meet you in the kitchen, if that's okay?"

He nodded again and watched mesmerized as she went up the stairs, ass swaying from side to side. The familiar feeling of desire he felt around her sparked to life. He wouldn't say he ran, but he did hurry into the kitchen before he did something stupid.

CHAPTER SIX

January 5th – Dusk

The fresh scent of coffee assailed her senses as she walked into the kitchen. She had to keep herself from drooling when she saw Thane leaning against the counter, chest gleaming, and a mug in his hand. He looked like he belonged there, filling her space and waiting for her. If only that were the reality.

She made a beeline for the pot and was stopped short when he handed her a cup she hadn't noticed before. She leaned against the counter opposite him so they could talk. The cup, warm in her hands, provided a distraction from the man in front of her.

Moments of silence slid by. "Feel better?" He rumbled out, his voice startling her. She had been staring down into the dark liquid wondering how to start a conversation with him.

"Better?"

"Now that you've checked on your brother."

"Oh, yeah. He's still sleeping. I forgot we didn't close the windows so he was huddled underneath the blankets. I closed everything up and don't expect we'll hear from him in a while. I'm hoping he'll sleep the rest of the night."

Thane grunted in reply. He did that a lot she noticed. It was like he wanted to say something but didn't want to offend her.

"You look wiped out."

"I am," she said without thinking. She looked up quickly. "You don't have to leave though." She heard the desperate edge in her voice. He had to have heard it as well. She may be tired, exhausted really, but she didn't want to be alone. Having Thane around made her feel safe. Let her think that, for a moment at least, she would be able to relax and not worry about anything. It was a very odd feeling. There had never been a time since her parents' death that she felt she could depend on someone, but she felt it with him.

He set his mug down on the countertop and crossed his arms over his chest. A golden eyebrow rose as he stared at her. "Drink your coffee," he said in quiet demand.

Bringing it to her lips, she sipped, humming as the hot brew went over her taste buds and down her throat. Her eyelids fluttered. It was damn near intoxicating. "Delicious."

"Thanks."

She studied him and noticed a slight blush to his cheeks. Had the compliment made him blush? She wouldn't embarrass him by asking. "I'm impressed. I didn't think a pretty boy like you would know how to make coffee. I imagined a housekeeper or girlfriend would do it for you." Yeah, she couldn't help but throw in that last part. Even though she had thought it all out earlier, it was entirely possible the man wasn't single.

"Beetah won't make my coffee. She says it will stunt my growth. She forgets that I'm a fully grown man."

"That doesn't sound like typical girlfriend behavior. I would guess most woman would do anything you asked without question."

"It isn't and she isn't. She's my housekeeper." He grinned at her, amusement twinkling in his eyes.

"Oh," she murmured, secretly thrilled by that nugget of information. He still didn't address the girlfriend comment and asking again would be prying. At least she thought it would seem that way, but she did have a right to know, especially at this point. Why she was being timid about it, she didn't know. He didn't stop her when she gave him a blowjob, and she hadn't bothered to ask. She wanted him...so she took him...simple as that.

Thane broke the silence that had descended on them again. "What are we going to do now?"

She tilted her head to the side and looked at him. "We? Now?"

"With your brother. You don't know what he's on."

"If anything at all," she interrupted. "Something is pulling him down there. I just don't know what. I refuse to believe its drugs. He doesn't have any signs of drug use."

"And you know what that looks like?"

Amara thought back to her parents' death, and the drugged-out lost soul that killed them for money. It didn't take long for the cops to find their killer. The guy shot both her mother and father, shoved her dad over, and drove the car to his dealer's house. The police, staking out the home, saw as he pulled up, waited for him to buy drugs, and then arrested the dealer and the druggie on the spot.

She had been the one the police contacted to identify the bodies and while she was there, she saw the man. If it had been within her power, she would have shot him dead on the spot.

"Yes," she said, but didn't elaborate.

Thane nodded, but didn't look convinced. "Okay. Whatever is going on with him, it has to be bad. He looks really sick. Like the life is being drained from him."

"There isn't anything I can do but wait and be there for him. I want to keep him in bed as much as possible and make sure he eats." *Maybe we can make it a sleepover and you can keep me in bed.*

He was completely unaware of her wayward thoughts. "It isn't going to be easy. He'll go through withdrawals of some type. Fight you to leave."

"How do you know?"

Thane shrugged and glanced away from her. "I've been around for a while. I've seen a lot of people go through some pretty bad shit." The air around him shimmered and peeked her curiosity.

"A while as in…"

He shook his head and clamped his lips tight.

So, he thought she would let him get away with not answering. Damn, did he have her all wrong! She couldn't stop the smile from forming on her face. She knew there was something about him that made him different. The old soul that lived in her body told her so — along with that radiant golden aura.

"Not answering isn't an option if you want to stick around."

"Who says I want to?" The snotty attitude rolled off him, getting under her skin. That was the man she had expected upon first seeing him. A man who wanted her to stroke his ego. Make it easier for him to stay.

Not happening.

Earlier she'd let her desperation bleed through. She wouldn't allow that to happen again. Straightening her spine, she set the cup down on the counter. In dramatic fashion, she waved her hand to the side. "Then, by all means, leave. I wouldn't want to keep you where you obviously don't want to be. The only prisoner here is my brother, and that's only because he's too weak to do anything about it. Give him time and he'll want to leave, and I'll let him."

Thane frowned and, dammit, even that looked sexy on him. "Amara?" he questioned. He reached for her and she batted his hand away. Hurt crossed his face and she caved much too quickly.

She released a long breath. "Listen, if you don't want to stay, then please just leave. I know you aren't what you seem, and if you don't want to answer my questions, I understand. I'd like to get to know you, but if that isn't what you want, it's okay. I thought there was an attraction between us, but hey — I've been known to be wrong. Just not often."

If at all possible, Thane's brows furrowed even more. He studied her silently, and she refused to react to it. Finally, he sighed, as if resigned to whatever decision he made. "Is there a place we can sit?"

She looked behind her at the family room connected to the kitchen. A large plush couch took center stage in the room, a leather ottoman and two small side tables strategically placed around it. The soft brown suede molded to the body, sucking you into its comfort.

Damn, it would feel good to kick back on it, but I'd probably fall right to sleep.

"Some place I won't be tempted to lay you down and fuck you."

"Oh!" He was interested then. Her heart sped up and beat wildly in her chest. Fragile feelings came to life and she knew if she let him, Thane would be a danger to her.

Grabbing his hand, she did her damndest to ignore the heat seeping into her at the touch. She dragged him to the back of the house out to the patio. Her sanctuary. The place she went to find her center and contemplate what to do next. It would be the best place to hear what he had to say. Plus, the patio furniture wasn't conducive to fooling around. Hard wicker and narrow cushions made for a horrible bed.

Night settled in around them once they walked out the backdoor. Crickets and frogs chirped, singing in the darkness. Flipping a switch, the wall-mounted gas lanterns lit, casting a soft glow over the landscape. It almost screamed romantic setting. A couple candles, some wine, and better seating and it would be. She wasn't out there for romance. She wanted answers.

Taking a deep breath, the clove scent of the Evening-Scented stock flowers planted around the patio washed over her, putting her at ease, as they always did. She motioned to the seat across from her, as she sat down and waited for Thane to get comfortable. He eased down into the narrow chair, dwarfing it with his tall frame. He frowned and shifted. It definitely wasn't comfortable for him. She suppressed the giggle trying to break free. "Where do you want to start?"

"To clear the air, I'm where I'm supposed to be."

Amara's eyebrows rose in surprise. What? "Supposed to be? As in, you aren't just a Good Samaritan, and we didn't meet by accident?"

"No, to both."

Amara scooted to the edge of her seat, ready to bolt back inside if need be. Not that she thought it would be necessary, but a girl couldn't be too careful. And now is a great time to realize that. After having him in your house…your shower…your mouth. "You better explain."

"When I said I've been around a while…I meant the past fifty years."

She gasped in shock. There wasn't a wrinkle on his too-handsome face. No gray hairs or sagging skin. "You don't look anywhere close to fifty."

He chuckled and it rankled her nerves. "I'm not. I'm more around 150, but then, that's fairly young for my kind."

If he expected her to laugh and call him a liar, he would be disappointed. It dawned on her she wasn't dealing with a normal man. She should have picked up on that tidbit earlier. She knew something was off but didn't put much thought into it. "You're a Mystic then."

Thane shifted in his seat. Eyes narrowing, he frowned in displeasure. "What do you know of Mystics?"

It was Amara's turn to flash a cocky grin. Finally, she had one up on him. "Are you admitting you're a Mystic?" She would find out what kind in due time. He wouldn't be the first one she'd run into. Being an Eternal, Mystics were drawn to the old soul within. She had counseled and guided many in her almost thirty years.

He dipped his head in acknowledgement. "Yes, now you answer my question. What do you know about them? And more importantly, how do you know about them?"

The 'what', in her opinion, would be easier to answer than the 'how'. Explaining how meant talking about her parents and her brother. That was something she needed to build up to. The hurt at their deaths was still too raw for her. She didn't think she would ever get over them being taken from her life at such an early age. They would miss so many things she and Deval would do over the years.

"Mystics are the lesser immortals that generally roam Earth. There are some lucky enough to live in the Heavens, the Underworld, or on Olympus. The Gods and Goddesses use all in some capacity, whether the Mystic knows it or not. I've mostly come across Shifters, Witches and Warlocks, and Vampires. The ones I've worked with have, for the most part, been pleasant and thankful for the guidance."

"Worked with," he gritted out.

She canted her head and tried to figure out the

reaction. What did he have to be irritated about? It wasn't like she needed his permission or protection from them. "Yes. I've worked with many Mystics. It's kind of my job."

His left eyebrow rose sharply. "When not hunting down your brother?"

She felt her cheeks flush. She hated letting those who depended on her down but, as usual, Deval had to come first. "Yes, there is that. I had to cancel all of my appointments this week so I could search for him. Hopefully, they can all wait for me to reschedule with them, or they will find another person to help."

"Why would they need your help in the first place? Is there a market for Mystic problems?"

The question felt like bait, and she wasn't quite ready to take it. "What do you need help with? What kind of Mystic are you?"

He looked affronted at her assumption. "Why do you think I need help? I'm fine. If anything, you're the one that could use help."

She nodded, conceding the point. She did need help for once and was grateful he had been there. That was a conversation for another time. "What are you? No, wait. Let me guess." Tapping her finger on her lips, she noticed she drew his attention there. His eyes glazed over and filled with heat. It would do well to distract him while she figured him out. Keep him from interrupting her.

She cleared her throat and started talking through her thoughts. "Let's see. You ventured into Viral City to look for me specifically, if what you say it true. Or you could have been there for Deval. I'm not sure which way I want to go with that yet."

His mouth opened then closed. Whatever he planned to say, he thought better of it.

She continued on. "That means you're brave, ignoring danger to your well-being. When you approached us in

67

the alley, I wasn't afraid. I instantly knew you would never do anything to harm my brother or me. You made me feel safe—protected. You were kind-hearted in your treatment of us both—even if you were disgusted by Deval's appearance and odor."

Rising from her seat, she walked to where he sat, stopping in front of him. He tracked her with his eyes, but the green depths gave nothing away. "You have an otherworldly glow about you—your aura. It's a soft golden halo that shimmers brighter when I'm near. I didn't notice it that much when we met, but the more I'm around you, the clearer it becomes. I generally don't see that in my clients. They'll have a haze around them, but color doesn't normally stand out."

Thane rose to his feet. Shifting closer, she felt the heat radiating off his bare chest. She looked him over from head to toe, but not like she'd done before. Not like she wanted to devour him inch by inch. Which she still wanted to do, but this wasn't the place for it. This time, she noticed his body in regards to being a Mystic. He was taller than the average man, taller than a good number of Mystics as well. In fact, he literally towered over her. His shoulders were broad and he was muscular, but not bulky in a gym rat kind of way. His waist was tapered. Body chiseled. While all Mystics tended to be on the pretty or handsome side, Thane appeared even more so. The clincher was his aura. It nagged at her until she stupidly realized what it meant. The golden hue was a nod to the Heavens.

Her lips spread into a wide smile. "I know what you are, and it's a first for me."

"Tell me," he said, his voice barely above a whisper. It traveled down her spine sending shivers in its wake.

Tilting her head back, their gazes collided. She licked her lips nervously or excitement. She didn't know which and, honestly, it didn't matter. The exhilaration at figuring out he was an angel quickly died a rapid death. Raw power surged through his eyes, making her weak in the knees. Holy shit! I gave a blowjob to, "an angel," she murmured in disbelief.

Her knees gave out under the impact of the realization and what that meant. Right before her world turned black, she felt Thane pluck her off her feet. There, in his protective grasp, she went the rest of the way under.

CHAPTER SEVEN

January 5th – Evening

Thane caught Amara right before she collapsed. The shock of figuring out what he was—apparently too much. He watched as she went from elation to horrified in a matter of seconds. Did the power he felt surge through his body have anything to do with her reaction? He had to admit, it was a new feeling for him. He could only guess it had something to do with getting closer to finishing his final task. Possibly the reemergence of his former abilities kick starting. He may have wings, but he wasn't flying anywhere. They were purely ornamental at this point.

Striding back into the house with Amara in his arms, he made his way straight to her bedroom.

Snuggled up against his chest, he was reminded of how small she was. Her soft, delicate features were relaxed. Her warm breath puffed against his chest. The sight invoked visions of endless nights of bringing her to bed after a long day. Having her curl her body next to his, resting her head on his chest while they talked about their day. Making love to relieve tension and connect on an elemental level before drifting off into sleep.

Maneuvering as best he could, Thane set Amara down on the bed. He pulled the sheets down on the opposite side, shifted her and repeated turning down the sheets on the other side. Shucking his pants, he crawled in next to her before covering them both with the bedding. He didn't know how long she would be out of it, but exhaustion tugged at him. Accustomed to getting regular sleep, his body wanted to shut down.

It was some time later when he woke up to Amara leaning over him. "I see you made yourself at home," she said softly.

Blinking rapidly, it took a minute for his eyes to adjust to the darkness of the room. A dim light from the bathroom cast a soft glow onto her pretty face. He saw the cute little smile playing at the corners of her mouth. His heart skipped a beat at the pleasure there. "Didn't want to leave you alone. You've had an emotional day, I didn't want it to be worse without me here."

"Oh, so for my welfare you slid into bed with me — naked?"

"Pants are overrated when it comes to sleeping." He could have left her when she'd fainted. Let her think the entire thing was her imagination. He didn't though. Without second-guessing his reasoning, he climbed into bed, wrapped his body around her, and drifted off to sleep. Best damn sleep he'd had in ages. The feel of her body missing was what drew him awake.

She snorted, then brushed a lock of hair off his forehead. The gentle touch was filled with more meaning than he cared to acknowledge. "I don't mind — angel."

"You remember then." It was a statement. He could see by the look on her face she didn't question what she thought she knew. In fact, she looked happy to have figured it out.

"Oh yeah. I know what it means and I'm okay with it

71

too. Explains a lot about why I've been drawn to you."

"You're my last task." An invisible weight lifted off his shoulders after telling her the truth. That had never been the case before. He always formed excuses for why he was with someone and why he had to disappear. "Your knowing will make this a hell of a lot easier." He hoped they could be on the same page. If she promised to stay inside and out of harm's way, or at least let him stick around until the end of the month, this would go a lot smoother. They might be able to enjoy each other while they waited the weeks out until she was taken to Olympus. He clued into the fact they weren't on the same page based on her reaction. His illusions of worry-free days and weeks of hot, uncomplicated sex flew out the window.

Her brows furrowed in confusion, then quickly smoothed. She laughed, the sound caressing his ears, sending a wave of arousal through him. It was soft and low. Like a woman warming up during foreplay, the build-up to throaty cries and guttural moans. His body took notice and responded appropriately, winding up in anticipation.

"Yes, but that's not all." She trailed her fingernails over his chest, skimming his skin, making it come alive. His dick twitched and became fuller. He was getting used to the reaction, though each time it responded, it felt more amazing than before.

"That's all." He grunted when her hand drifted over his rising cock before cupping his balls, rolling them gently. The resulting tingle had his eyes rolling into the back of his head.

"Nope, that isn't all," she purred.

He meant to counter her, completely confused about what else there could be, but he couldn't. The scrape of her nails over his balls had him spreading his legs apart, giving her more room to play. Soft lips landed on his chest. She hummed against his skin between licks, nips, and kisses. The vibrations traveling down his stomach and landing in the balls she still fondled.

Damn, she made him hard. Granted, it had been ages, but this…her, the reason he was even with her, and the light at the end of the tunnel…it made it better than ever.

Nimble fingers fluttered over his aching dick, playing with the head before she ringed them, sliding them down. Her grip was firm and torturous. Exactly the way he liked it. Covers were pushed down his body as she blazed a path with her lips in the same direction. She nibbled on his hipbones. Left a wet trail to his bellybutton and placed soft, sucking kisses all over him on the way to his cockhead. He bucked beneath her, lifting them both off the mattress when she scraped her teeth over the sensitive head and back up, then greedily gobbled him down.

She toyed with him. Laving the delicate skin, then firmly stroking with her hand. She repeated the action, moaning deeply. The slick sound of her fingers on her flesh reached his ears. She was fingering herself. Getting off on what she was doing to him, making his dick even harder.

She wouldn't be getting off by her own power again. Not this time. He would have a hand in making her come, and preferably when he was thrust so far into her she'd never let him go.

Pushing her off him, he grabbed her under her arms and pulled her up over his face. Her hands landed on the wall as he placed her knees on either side of his head. Without finesse, he dove in with his tongue, keeping his arms anchored over her thighs. The scent of her arousal flowed around him, tempting him further.

Tonguing her from top to bottom, he sucked in as much of her juices as he could. The sweet nectar slid down his throat, pulling a groan from his chest. She tasted of jasmine and feminine musk. She tasted perfect. Nibbling on her clit, he worked an arm between them, screwing a finger into her tight, little cunt. Stroking in and out a couple times before she grunted. "More."

Never one to deny a lady, another finger joined the first. She wiggled and squirmed above him, his name falling from her lips. He wanted her on the edge before he shoved his cock into her. It had been too long since he'd gotten off inside a woman, and he knew this first time wouldn't even come close to making up for it. He also wouldn't last long given the way her pussy clamped down tightly on his digits.

Her legs quivered around his head and he knew she was close. A man never forgot what it felt like to have a woman shatter around him. Abruptly he pulled his fingers from her. She gasped and pushed away from the wall at about the same time he grabbed her by the waist, pulling her onto her back between his legs. Scrambling to get on top of her, he was halted by one little word.

"Condom," she breathed out.

He groaned in agony. It may have been fifty years, but he was well aware of the latex. He had watched enough porn to grasp the concept and application. Humans used it to prevent disease and unwanted pregnancy. He could have told her he was clean and would never get any of the human sexually transmitted diseases, but he didn't want to delay his getting inside her pussy longer than necessary.

She rolled to the side, presenting her pretty backside to him as she rummaged in her nightstand. Her long hair, still braided, snagged his attention and inspiration hit.

Gripping her waist, he scooted up close, allowing his cock to rest between the globes of her ass. The contrast between his angry red cock and her delicious brown skin a complete turn-on. His erection jumped against her, begging to be let in. Knowing that would happen soon, he opted to torture them both while she searched for protection. He didn't want to stop moving. All too afraid this was a dream and he would snap out of it before they could go further.

Angling his penis down, he let it run between the lips of her sex. Thrusting slowly back and forth, hitting her clit on every return. She moaned, and he kept at it until she tossed the condom at him.

With speed and efficiency he didn't know he possessed, he ripped open the package, got the latex on, and entered her in one swift, powerful move. He groaned deeply and she cried out. Her head thrown back, he was reminded of his plan.

First he had to wait to allow the overwhelming sensation of being inside a woman to pass. Her inner muscles flexed, griping him. Massaging him. His hand tightened on her hip to hold her at bay. "Wait," he gritted out. "Been too long."

She didn't heed his warning and, instead, rocked gently, easing them into a rhythm and ramping him up. Snagging her braid, he wrapped it around his fist, pulled her head back until she moaned, then eased out slowly before slamming in again, taking control. They both groaned in pleasure, and it didn't take long before he was slamming into her over and over again.

She dropped her chest to the bed, and he gave her the slack to go down. Questing fingers flitted around his cock, and he knew she was going to rub her clit, bring herself to orgasm. If it had been any other time, he would have batted her hand away and done it himself. This first time though, they both needed to reach the pinnacle — and soon.

Her moan, low and keening, was music to his ears. Her moist heat fluttered around him before seizing him in a tight grip. "Fuck." Thane came before he knew he was ready. The swift rush from his balls taking over. Gripping her hips hard, he ground against her as he filled the condom, irritated that he couldn't feel her flesh on his, and the searing heat of her pussy as she pulled him under.

Sitting back on his heels, he slid out of her. Amara collapsed to the bed and groaned. "Now that was worth waiting for."

Thane chuckled. With care he climbed off the bed and went to the bathroom to take care of the condom and clean up. He came back out with a warm washcloth, wiped Amara clean, and tossed it in the laundry basket.

As he walked back into the bedroom, he noticed something different about her. A soft golden haze formed around her luscious body — a haze that wasn't there before.

Amara rolled onto her back and waited for Thane to come back to bed. She exhaled and allowed the blissful afterglow to flow through her. It had been too long since she'd fucked. Since she had felt a man's lips on her body. His fingers in her pussy. His determination to be the one to bring her to orgasm.

That it was Thane, a fallen angel, who did it, was just a bonus. He may think of her as only his last task, but she knew better. It was time to have a real conversation with the man. Now that their lust was sated.

He stopped a couple steps into her room and looked at her strangely. His brows furrowed and lips pinched. The urge to laugh nearly overtook her. The poor man, he had no idea what was really going on.

From past experience, and teachings from her mother, Amara knew the Gods and Goddesses enjoyed playing with their minions, or who they perceived to be theirs. It was never more evident than now.

Thane roaming her world meant he had been banished from his home. It didn't matter to her where he came from. The Heavens. The Underworld. Or, more likely, Olympus. He'd had an air of superiority earlier in that alley with Deval. A holier than thou kind of attitude. Airs like that didn't bother her. She knew those from a world other than hers thought they were better. They either learned they were not or they seethed in anger; becoming spiteful, cruel beings that didn't last long.

"Come back to bed, Thane," she called out softly. "It'll be more comfortable while we talk"

He nodded sharply, seeming to come to the same conclusion. Lying down, he held out his arm, offering a place to snuggle. She crawled up next to him and got comfortable, resting her head and hand on his chest and belly. The feel of his warm, strong body next to hers made her never want to leave his side. There was comfort with him she hadn't experienced before.

His sigh of contentment echoed what she felt and had her smiling against his skin. He pulled the covers over them, creating a cocoon of warmth. "Where should we start?" he rumbled out.

"What do you want to know?" she asked. Not sure diving right into her background was the way to go. It would be better to let him lead the discussion.

"Let's go back to how you know about Mystics."

Amara made little circles on his belly with her finger. Something to keep her hand busy while they talked. Maybe distract him a little when it came time to reveal what the big picture was. "I've known about the existence of Mystics since childhood."

He tensed slightly beneath her. He took in a deep breath and then released it out, the tension going with it. "I find that hard to believe. How is that possible?"

"It's rather simple really, if you think about it. How does one know all of the secrets of the world when they are not a God or Goddess?"

"All of the secrets of the world?" Skepticism bled through his words. She didn't know what his knowledge of Mystics and others like her was.

"Maybe not all of them, but a good portion." She pushed away from his body and sat up. It would be better to look him in the eyes. His response paramount to how they proceeded. "I'm an Eternal."

Thane shoved up to a sitting position as well, leaning back against the headboard. He grinned brightly, amusement lighting his eyes. "I know that, little one." He plucked up her hand and pulled her closer. "Figured that out when I got the assignment. That can't be all of it though. While an Eternal has an immortal soul, they are not all knowing."

Amara couldn't stop her frown. Here she thought she had a leg up on him and she didn't. She would in a second though. "Okay mister smarty-pants, did you know this? My mother was a progeny of the Muse Clio. Because of that, she passed down the knowledge and teachings of history she knew. Well, as much as she could before she died."

It was his turn to frown. "I didn't know that. If she was a progeny, why didn't she live on Olympus?"

Now she understood the look on his face. "You tell me. You were banished from Olympus, weren't you?"

"Temporarily removed," he said, his tone haughty.

"That explains your belief that it is the end all, be all when it comes to places to live. I assure you…it isn't. Life here with the regular folk is pretty good too. To answer your question, though, not all progeny live on Olympus. They can choose where they want to be and whom they want to be with. As for my mother, she said it was love at first sight when she met my father. She was sent to work with him at his job as a Historian. They married and made their life here. It was a twist of fate that my brother and I are Eternals. It had to be because of the twin thing and mother's relationship to Clio, I'm guessing."

"That would make sense. Why did you say 'that's not all' when I mentioned you being my last task? What else could there be?"

Amara scooted up next to him. The need to touch him while they talked weighed down on her, making it impossible to resist. Tucking herself up under his arm, she wiggled to get comfortable before going back to drawing circles on his chest. Sweeping her finger lightly around his flat brown nipple, she scraped her nail across it. The flesh

78

puckered and held her attention. "There is actually quite a lot more to it, but I'm not sure you're ready to handle it."

He snorted in typical male fashion when told he couldn't do something. The hand he had wrapped around her shoulders slid down her back. Next she knew he was tugging on her braid, attempting to pull her head up. She wouldn't budge. "Try me."

"How long has it been since you've had sex?"

The question must have stunned him. The tugging on her braid stopped momentarily before starting again when he spoke. "Since I've been here. About fifty years."

"And all of this time, you've never once felt desire for anyone else?"

"No."

"Did you wonder why, all of a sudden, you did with me?" She tilted her head back and sneaked a glance at him. His eyes were hooded, guarding his emotions. Whether protecting her or him, she wasn't sure.

He shrugged. "I figured I was close to finishing my task."

Nodding her head slightly, she agreed. "It's more than that though. I may not have been around for many physical years, but my soul has and with it the memories. A final tasking of a Grigori is never as simple as it seems. You've done something to offend someone and, with your lusty nature, it had to involve sex. What did they tell you about me? What did they say you needed to do?"

"To keep you from doing something stupid. I have to say, sleeping with a man you just met might be considered stupid, and that means I've failed us both."

Amara couldn't stop from laughing. "I have never done anything stupid, and that includes having sex with you."

"You were down in Viral City looking for your
79

brother. I tracked you for three days, making sure nothing happened."

That had her spine stiffening. She'd felt eyes on her when she was down there, but was never able to figure out where it was coming from. At the time, she figured it was paranoia. He tugged her braid, and she felt him pulling off the band on the end. Inch by inch he loosened it, sifting his fingers through her hair. The feel of his hand working away, slowly relaxed her. She loved when a man played with her hair. It made her scalp tingle, which released endorphins. Which, in turn, made her horny. Such a slippery slope she was on, but there was much more they needed to discuss.

"I was never in danger down there. I know how to handle myself, and there was never a threat."

"So I saw. It was still stupid and, in keeping with my task, I had to get you out of there. I wished to lock you away until the end of the month."

The way his eyes glazed over with lust made her think there was more. "Just lock me away," she said, her voice husky with arousal.

"Or tie you to my bed," he said begrudgingly.

To reward him for telling her that; she leaned forward and licked his nipple while she played with the other. A soft groan puffed across her hair, and his hand tightened on her scalp. After a few seconds, she released him. "And your response to me is nothing more than that—a response? The hot sex would happen with anyone?"

The fingers digging into her scalp guided her head lower. "I don't know what you're getting at," he grumbled when she bit him in the side, startling him enough to let go of her head.

She moved away from him and stared him down. "A Grigori's final task is never as simple as sitting on your ass keeping someone from doing something stupid. That would be too easy. What do you see when you look at me?

What do you feel?"

He didn't answer. He sat there glaring at her, lips pinched in irritation.

She let him stew in his own thoughts. Hopping off the bed, she went to the bathroom and tossed on a robe. She needed to check on Deval, and the break from Thane's stubbornness was much needed. She walked back into the bedroom but didn't move closer to him. She wanted to. Desperately. But if he didn't figure it out on his own, he would never get to go home.

"Think it all over, Thane. What would make Zeus let you come back to Olympus after all these years? What would he demand from you to ensure whatever it was you did, did not happen again? That is how you'll figure it all out. Sadly, I know the answer but it can't come from me. It is something you need to figure out and believe in your heart."

CHAPTER EIGHT

January 6th – Morning

Amara woke up alone in bed after the first restful
night she'd had in ages. Thane's warm body cocooned her
for most of the night. Lulling her into a sense of security
she hadn't felt in years. She wished she'd been able to
wake up next to him while he was still asleep. She wanted
to study him openly. Trace his features with her fingers.
Skim her hands over the hard planes of his body. Draw
him from slumber with soft kisses that lead to hot, sweaty
monkey sex.

A girl could always do with rough dirty sex in the
morning. It got the blood pumping…among other things.

She smiled and closed her eyes. "If wishes were
pennies…I'd be one rich woman."

Knowing deep down inside she wouldn't find him
in her home, she still scanned the room, hoping to prove
her inner instincts wrong. But they weren't, she didn't see
anything. Literally — nothing. His pants were gone and so
was his T-shirt. She knew if she looked in her bathroom,
his shoes would be missing as well.

The fresh brewed scent of coffee didn't linger in the air, and the only sound in the house came from the ticking of the cuckoo clock in the office library.

"I guess he decided he didn't want what the Gods were offering." A small shard of hurt tried to pierce her heart, but she refused to let it. Things had a way of working out exactly as the Fates deemed. Causing herself undue heartache would solve nothing.

Rolling out of bed, Amara made quick work of cleaning up and getting dressed for the day. She pulled on grungy sweats and an old T-shirt, then made her way into the kitchen. She didn't need to look decent for anyone, least of all Deval. She doubted he would notice her to begin with. One good night's sleep wouldn't cure what ailed him. Not this quickly.

A fresh pot of coffee on, she made the decision to forget about Thane and concentrate on her brother. He would need all of her attention if she were going to nurse him back to health. He would also keep her mind from drifting toward the man who didn't want what she offered.

CHAPTER NINE

January 9th – Mid-morning

Three days later a heavy knock sounded on her door. Without thought she ran down the stairs, whipping the door open before bothering to check to see whom it was. She didn't stop to think that no one should be knocking on her door. Not even delivery drivers did. They buzzed and she checked credentials before letting them through the gate.

Thane stood on her doorstep, hands shoved into his front pockets, luggage sitting next his leg, and a frown plastered on his face. Anger glittered in the green depths of his eyes.

She heaved an irritated breath. She didn't have time for his anger at whatever he perceived she'd done wrong. Deval had woken minutes before, thrashing and crying out. She barely got him calmed down before she heard the knock. "What are you doing here and how did you get through the gate?"

"What are you doing opening the door before asking who's there? I could have been a mass murderer."

"Can someone be labeled a mass murderer when there are only two people in the house," she quipped.

He dropped his head back and groaned. "Why?" he asked. "Why her?"

She rolled her eyes and started to close the door.

His hand shot out stopping her. "Oh no you don't." Digging in his pocket, he pulled out a set of keys. Pressing a button, a bird-like chirp sounded from her driveway.

Sticking her head out the door, she noticed an expensive car parked near the garage.

Duh, how else would he get a giant ass suitcase here?

Her attention was drawn back to the luggage. "What are you doing, moving in?" She crossed her arms beneath her breasts. Thane's gaze dropped from her face to her chest. She was by no means ample in that area, so she wasn't wearing a bra. She glanced down and saw the way her breasts were plumped and her nipples puckered, pushing against the soft cotton of the shirt she had on.

She snapped her fingers. "Hey, eyes up here. What are you doing with that?" She pointed to the bag next to him.

One of his golden eyebrows rose, and the corner of his mouth curved up. He had that you-should-know-the-answer look on his face. "You didn't think I'd given up already, did you?"

Heat rushed over her cheeks. She did a one-shoulder shrug kind of thing and kept her lips sealed.

"You did. Sorry to burst your bubble, little one, but I'm here to stay. I had to take care of a few things, and then had an unexpected visitor I couldn't convince to leave. He's probably eating me out of house and home as we speak." The last part came out muttered and filled with affectionate irritation.

As much as she wanted to talk about what that was about, she had other priorities.

85

Thane stepped forward and kissed her. The softness and sweetness of the kiss melted a tiny bit of the ice around her heart that had started to form since he left. He brushed his mouth over hers again and again until she responded. Her hands landed on his chest, gripping his shirt to hold on as her head spun. The man overwhelmed her even when he was taking his time.

A cry from inside the house stopped her in her tracks. She pushed away from Thane, spinning on her heel, and dashed back upstairs without a word. Vaguely she heard the front door close and booted footsteps follow behind her.

As she wrestled Deval back onto his bed, she couldn't stop the tripping of her fickle heart when Thane stepped in to help her out.

There was going to be an internal battle as long as Thane was in her home. Part of her wanted to fall at his feet and ask him to be the shoulder she leaned on. The other part of her told her to guard her heart because it was in mortal danger.

CHAPTER TEN

January 15th – Mid-afternoon

Thane had essentially moved in with her. He shared her bed at night and responsibilities during the day. Amara took in the sight of her bedroom. "And he's taken over my room," she said in wonder. His clothes were strewn about on random pieces of furniture. The suitcase long since unpacked and shoved into the back of her closet.

After the Friday he showed back up at her door, the weekend and the following week were spent taking shifts watching over Deval. The worst of the night terrors had eased by Tuesday. He spent more hours awake as each day went by. He ate more and even got out of bed, though she insisted he stay on the second floor of the house. He was still weak in her opinion, and she didn't want him falling down the stairs. Amara had a feeling Deval's progress had a lot to do with Thane and the angelic powers he gained back daily. His ability to instill calm and serenity was a true gift from the Gods.

With Deval on the mend and Thane there to help, Amara started back to work, and her first appointment would be showing up in a couple of minutes. It was decided that she should work from home, putting the office library to an actual use. It didn't take much, and Thane happily agreed to the proposal. He kept watch over her, which eased both of their minds.

The doorbell rang, startling her. She grabbed the sweater she came looking for and walked hastily to the door. As per Thane's insistence, she took a second to look out the window next to the door. Not that she would know what this client looked like. He was new to her, requesting an appointment through her online service. The man at the door looked at her and smiled. Her breath caught in her throat in surprise. He was taller than Thane, muscular and, holy hell, good looking. His brown hair glimmered in the wintery sunlight and his dark eyes twinkled with mischief.

His deep voice poured through the door. "I'm here to see Ms. Hope. My name is Gabe. I made an appointment with your service." Their gazes locked and she got lost. There was buzzing in her ears, her head spun. "Miss Hope?" He queried, breaking her from the spell she'd been under.

She flushed and unlocked the door, ushering him inside. "I'm so sorry. You're just so…tall," she said meekly. She couldn't tell him he was gorgeous. That would be unprofessional and something else she couldn't quite put her finger on.

Thane came loping down the stairs as she led Gabe into her office. When the two men locked onto one another, Thane's eyes narrowed and she thought she heard Gabe chuckle.

Amara chose to ignore the alpha male posturing. "My three o'clock appointment is here, Thane. I'll be in my office for the next hour." In the library, she sat in one of the overstuffed leather chairs. Sinking into the supple material, she enjoyed a few moments of relaxed silence before Gabe joined her.

That asshole.

Thane prowled the hallway outside the office library, passing the doorway every few seconds. His teeth grinding as Gabriel laughed in the other room. What the fuck was he doing here? His friend had no right to invade Amara's space.

'You didn't either,' the little voice in his head retorted. But he did have a right. Amara was his. At least that's what he told himself. He still hadn't gotten up the nerve to discuss their relationship.

Over the past week he'd shared her bed and her life. She was loving and quick to forgive. She put her all into everything, even though most of it didn't benefit her in the slightest. She spent countless hours keeping watch over her brother. Cleaning him up. Feeding him. Nurturing him.

Thane could imagine she would be like that with their children as well. Praising them for every little accomplishment. Comforting them when they were hurt, whether physically or mentally. Being there when they needed her most and standing by when they thought they didn't.

An all too familiar ache speared his chest. He admired Amara. Wanted to spend his every waking moment with her. Spend more nights staring at the stars with her while he held her in his arms. The sex was great, but the quiet times enjoying each other's company was addictive.

None of that would happen, though, unless he convinced her to come with him back to Olympus. A part of him thought she would do it. He'd seen the tender expression on her face as she gazed at him when she didn't think he was looking. He felt the tight grasp of her arms around his body at night, like she thought he would disappear when the morning came.

Could he do it? It would be selfish of him, but when had he not been?

Gabriel's chuckle echoed loudly in the hall again, getting on his last nerve. The hour was almost up, and he couldn't take her being in the same room with his friend another minute. Not wanting to look like a complete fool though, he marched into the kitchen and poured Amara a cup of coffee.

Taking a deep breath, he strolled into the office, interrupting — fully intending on breaking the party up. Only he was the one that got the surprise. Amara and Gabe were standing, her delicate hand in his large grip. She smiled up at him and when he thought about it later, he would say it was clearly professional on her part. At the moment, the way Gabriel looked at Amara, it enraged him. Gabe looked like he wanted to devour her. The heat in his eyes giving away how he felt.

He cleared his throat noisily and brushed past them both. Calmly, at least he hoped it looked that way, he set the coffee cup on the table next to the leather chair. Sidling up to Amara, he wrapped his arm around her shoulder, tucking her in close.

Gabriel's dark brow rose in question, as a smirk spread across his face. Never in Thane's life had he wanted to beat the shit out of his friend more than he did at that moment.

Amara shot daggers at him through narrowed eyes. She could be angry at his behavior all she wanted. It would only make for great sex once Gabriel left, and after he chastised her for touching another man.

"Thank you for seeing me, Amara." Her name rolled off Gabriel's tongue sex-filled and husky.

Out of the corner of his eye, he watched to see what her reaction would be. Her brows furrowed in confusion and she pulled her hand from his.

A small jolt of pride raced through him to see that she didn't succumb to the sound. Thane could say for a fact, she was the first woman to ever not fall under Gabriel's spell.

"You're welcome," she said. She licked her lips nervously as she looked between Gabriel and him.

"I'll walk him to the door, little one. Have a seat and drink your coffee." He turned her toward him, pulling her into his arms. He gave her a second to pull away and when she didn't, he kissed her senseless. Sure, a small part of him did it to prove something to Gabe, but really he did it for himself. He needed to assert control over the situation and prove she belonged to him.

Gabriel chuckled, breaking them apart. "I'll see myself out. You two have fun." He grinned and left without another word. Thane heard the front door shut but didn't feel relief.

If anything, the resounding thud of the door edged him closer to madness. A panic enveloped him that he had never felt before. Damn, with this woman, he felt more in less than a month than he had the previous 150 years.

For an hour she kept company with a man who, with the crook of a finger, had any woman he wanted. If given the chance, Gabriel would have tried to take Amara from him.

No, he wouldn't let it happen, but he would be taking...Amara over her desk, reminding her whom she belonged to.

Through an assault of kisses, he navigated them to her desk. Never in his life had he been so happy to live with a neat freak. This wouldn't be a long, slow loving of her body. She would probably appreciate that. The past week he learned she enjoyed her sex anyway it came.

He nibbled his way down her throat, pausing on her rapid pulse at the base of her neck. It did crazy things to him to know it sped up just for him. That he created such a rush in her that her heart beat out of control and her pulse fluttered like a butterfly trying to take off.

Spinning her around, he pushed her up against the desk, leaning over her, rubbing his hard-on against her

91

backside. Her groaned yes the only thing he needed to hear before lifting her too prim skirt up.

With one hand on her lower back, he used his other to pull his shirt off over his head, tossing it onto the desk next to her. He unbuttoned his jeans, unzipped his zipper, and shoved his pants down enough to get his cock free. Supremely glad they'd had the condom and birth control discussion, and deciding going bare was fine, he shifted her thong to the side and entered her in one swift move. The sudden invasion causing her to catch her breath. Not taking the time, because he didn't think he could, he retreated; then thrust into her again…moving at a hurried pace. The heat of her pussy wrapped around him. The intensity of what he was feeling almost too much to bear.

She cried out his name. Her voice sounded desperate and needy. He slipped a hand around her hip and didn't stop until he felt her clit beneath his fingers. Quick, hard circles, followed by rough taps to the hardened nub made her inner muscles quiver. He needed her grasping his dick like she never wanted to let him go.

A flash of her standing there smiling up at Gabriel crossed his mind. The sight made him dig his fingers harder into the hip he held and put more pressure on her clit. Anger and arousal warred within, ending in a draw when he growled out her name. Whether he was declaring it to her or the Gods above, he didn't know.

"Mine," he grunted, slamming into her. "Always. Mine."

Her pussy fluttered and seized, clamping down on his cock shuttling in and out of her. It was all he needed to push him over the edge.

On a roar he came inside her, filling her with his seed. It was only an afterthought that he wished she could actually become pregnant with his child.

CHAPTER ELEVEN

January 23rd – Evening

Amara waited for Thane to join her on the patio. It had been a long, stressful week for them both. Deval was more mobile, now staying up during the day, moping around the house. He wouldn't talk to them about what had happened, but at every turn she could feel his desire to leave. That unbreakable bond of being twins was finally broken. It hurt her heart, but she held out hope that they could fix it. That she could fix him. If only he would talk to her. Give her a chance.

A sound from the family room had her turning her heard. Thane stood talking to Deval, their voices too soft to hear. Whatever they talked about, they didn't want her to know and, at this point, she didn't think she cared. She only wanted to spend more time with Thane in her little bubble of happiness. In one more week he would leave her.

They didn't talk about his task and what it meant. They actively avoided the subject when Deval asked Thane why he was at the house. Even Deval knew there was more to the relationship than they were letting on.

Turning back around, she sighed and reached for her glass of wine. She was already on her second one. It was that kind of night. She sipped the tart, heady blend and relaxed into the lounger.

She and Thane spent so much time on the patio, they decided they needed much more comfortable furniture. Pieces that would be conducive to heavy petting and slow, luxurious sex. Once it had been delivered, they wasted no time in trying it out in every conceivable way.

It wasn't until Thane sat down at the end of the lounger that she realized she'd zoned out. He picked up her foot and rubbed little circles into the ball. She moaned with pleasure. "You okay, little one?"

She nodded and sipped her wine. Saluting him, she said, "Getting better by the minute."

He chuckled and eyed her speculatively.

So, she took up the middle of the seat and didn't leave room for him. He'd get over it. Plucking the wine glass from her fingers and setting it down, he then picked her up and made himself comfortable on the seat with her on his lap. Reaching over, he grabbed her glass and handed it back. "That's better," he said gruffly.

Settling into the silence, Amara soaked in the feel of Thane. His strength and caring for her making her want to cry at times. Her heart knowing it would end too soon. She sipped down the rest of her wine.

He took it from her without asking and set it aside. He did things like that more and more. If she needed help getting a dish down, he was there to grab it. If things were too tough with Deval, he sent her downstairs to rest, taking over the care of her brother. One time he even attempted to cook dinner. That didn't turn out too well, but she appreciated the effort.

The biggest nod to how much he had changed since

she first met him was their bedroom. He picked up all of his clothes and neatly stacked them away in the few drawers she'd cleaned out for him. He hung his shirts and made space on the counter for his stuff in the bathroom.

The entire business of him being in her life felt personal. He felt like the man she was falling in love with.

Nestling her head on his shoulder, she leaned in and kissed his neck. He squeezed her but didn't do anything more. He must have known she only wanted comfort. "Tell me a story," she said softly. "Something to take my mind off all my worries."

"Anything for you, little one," he said before kissing her sweetly.

She signed again, but this time in contentment, and allowed his voice to wash over her. It didn't matter what the words were or what the story was about. She just wanted to listen to him talk. Soak up as much of him as she could before she inevitably had to say goodbye.

As Thane rumbled on about a good friend of his seducing one of Thane's former housekeepers, she drifted off to sleep. Secure in the thought that he would be there to hold her through the night for at least a couple more nights.

CHAPTER TWELVE

January 30th

A piece of Amara's soul broke off and shattered as she silently watched Deval sneak out of the house. Heavy coat wrapped around him. Thick boots on his feet. He had taken the fat roll of money from her purse and left without a word. She didn't care that he took the money. She put it there for him because she knew this would happen. What she cared about was his compulsion to leave her. She cared that he didn't talk to her, that he believed he needed to be in Viral City.

In the weeks since he'd been home, he'd gained back at least twenty pounds. He was rested and physically stronger, but no less secretive about where he had been and why he had left. The only thing he told her was that he had no choice. That his calling was to be back on the streets. His promise to not let it get as bad did little to ease her worries.

Thane wrapped his arms around her chest, pulling her back into his solid body. She melted into him, siphoning off his heat and strength. She was so damn tired emotionally...physically. She could thank Thane for the last. The night before, she could feel Deval slipping away and in desperation to hold onto something, she seduced her all too willing lover.

"You have to let him go, Amara," she said quietly.

"I know," she said, a hitch catching in her throat. "This isn't something I can fix, is it?"

Thane pressed a kiss onto the top of her head. "No. I'm sorry, little one. He is on his own path, and there is nothing that can change his course. He'll be okay though. With time, he'll find what he's looking for."

Her heart ached hearing his words, but she knew he was right. The demons chasing Deval were his and his alone. Amara could only hope he found a way out of this downward spiral soon. It was time to let him go...just as it was time to let Thane go.

A reassuring squeeze from Thane had her bringing her head up. Deval had made it to the end of the driveway, and he looked back at the house. Their eyes locked and he nodded once. The stark sadness she saw in his killed her.

Sighing she turned into Thane's chest. She would have to say goodbye all over again...and soon. There was one day left in the month and their time was up. He'd packed his suitcase earlier while she spied on her brother. She didn't think he knew she had seen him. He tucked the bag away in her closet, probably as to not upset her.

She'd ridiculously fallen in love with her fallen angel, though it appeared he had not fallen in love with her. There were moments when she thought he would profess how he felt, but it didn't happen. Those moments when they were caught up in the blissful aftermath of making love, or sitting on the patio late at night merely breathing the same cool air. He was affectionate and playful. He couldn't keep his hands off her and vice versa. Who would want to when he traipsed around her house in nothing but jeans, top button undone. He tempted her on so many levels it wasn't funny.

Then there was his intelligence, sarcastic wit, and ability to make her laugh. He regaled her with stories from his years on Olympus. The way the inhabitants played sneaky games and joked with each other. He was well versed with the goings-on of the world, politically and socially. They didn't run out of things to talk about; and yet, they didn't feel the need to fill all of the empty space with noise.

The comfort she felt around him, she didn't think she'd feel around any other man. She was seriously, unequivocally, in love with him.

How unfortunate for her.

"Let's go sit down, you look dead on your feet." Thane maneuvered her into the family room, gently pushing her toward the couch. He walked off into the kitchen and brewed some coffee. As he waited, he leaned against the counter, his gaze focused out the back windows. Did he wonder how he was going to tell her he was leaving? Should she make it easy on him?

The whole reason he was in her home came crashing to the forefront. He had succeeded and yet failed in his task—all at the same time. Unless you considered falling in love with him stupid, which she didn't...only foolhardy. Hopefully, Zeus would allow him back on Olympus regardless. If there was a way to get word to him to plead Thane's case, then she would. She would promise anything to give Thane what he thought was his heart's one true desire. It wasn't his fault he didn't fall madly in love with her. That rested solely on her shoulders. She wasn't the woman to capture his love. The Gods had gotten it wrong.

Thane stared out the window hoping for divine intervention. The woman he desired above all others sat close by with a heavy heart, and he needed to find a way to leave without hurting her more. Her brother's departure couldn't have come at a worse time. But then, there wasn't a good time for someone you loved to leave without a word, which is why he had to find the words.

Tomorrow Gabriel would let him know if he was returning home — to Olympus. A part of him, a large part, wanted to beg Amara to come with him, to stay with him. Somehow find a way to make her give up her life and become his.

He thought about the words from that first night after they had sex. For weeks on end he tried to figure out the puzzle, which was laid before him. One night, as she slept curled up next to him, he realized the only way Zeus would allow him back was if Thane fell in love. For once, an angel believed in love, had been loved and loved another; he could touch no one else. It was a curse and a blessing.

He refused to tell Amara the words he knew she wanted to hear. He didn't want to rip her from all she knew for his own selfish reasons. He loved her, body and soul. He finally understood what it meant to think of someone else. Little good that did him now.

Pouring two cups of coffee, he carried them to where Amara sat. She smiled softly at him, a look of understanding in her eyes. He shook his head at his ignorance. Of course she would know what he was about to do. She had proven time and again more intelligent than her physical age. He set the cups on the side table and gathered her in his arms. He tucked his face into the crook of her neck, breathing in her jasmine scent, hoping to imprint it on his own tattered soul.

She combed her fingers through his hair, soothing him. "It's okay, Thane. I know you need to leave," she said, her voice serene.

He opened his mouth but was stopped from speaking with a finger on his lips. "Shhh...don't say something you'll regret later. I have enjoyed having you with me these last few weeks. I don't know what I would have done if you hadn't been there to help me pick up the pieces, or Deval for that matter. I would have crumbled under the stinky weight of him and died a most noxious death."

He chuckled, knowing she was trying to lighten the mood. The ache in his heart wouldn't go away though. He squeezed her tight and kissed her neck. Nuzzling her neck, he decided to express with his body what he couldn't say with words. He tumbled her to the couch, covering her with his much larger body. Clothes flew to the ground until they both lay naked and panting.

Their lovemaking was slow and reverent. He showered kisses over her entire body. Savoring the taste of her lips…her skin. He worked his way down her body until he was at the apex of her thighs. He breathed her in, letting her scent infuse his lungs. He would need to remember this moment — the look, the feel, the taste…for the rest of his immortal life.

He set his mouth against her dark pussy lips, tasting her, drinking her in. She squirmed beneath him, her hand threading through his hair. Tilting her hips, she pressed harder against his face, demanding he give her more. He did, but only for a little bit. He thrust two fingers in her, pumping into her flesh while sucking hard against her clit. She shivered and shifted, grinding up against him. He pulled back at the last minute, then climbed over her body, settling between her thighs. Kissing her deeply, he let her taste her honey on his lips. She hummed as her tongue tangled with his, capturing it in her mouth. She mimicked the fucking she wanted. Too bad he wasn't inclined to give it to her.

He needed to savor this last moment with her, and he would do it slowly, giving him time to memorize each and every aspect.

As she sucked his tongue, he gradually fed his cock into her. The slow slide sending shudders down his back. She arched beneath him, breaking her lock on his tongue. Planting his hands next to her head, her eyes were glazed over in pleasure and her mouth open wide on a silent

100

moan. He drove into her slowly, only picking up speed when her pussy rippled against him. It took two or three more thrusts with him grinding against her core before she went over the edge in orgasm. His name burst from her lips and he followed her into ecstasy.

I love you, Amara. He allowed to words to race across his brain, but refused to speak them. He wouldn't burden her with his love and a no-win situation.

In silence they cleaned up and got dressed. He pulled his suitcase from her closet and she walked him to the door. When she went to follow him outside, he stopped her. It would be difficult as it was, and he wanted to know she was safe inside her house as he drove off.

Leaning down he kissed her. Pouring all of his love into it then pulled away. She gripped his shirt, her knuckles white. His mouth opened then closed. What more could he say to her? What could he say that would ease her pain? Swallowing hard, he knew there was no answer.

He turned and started walking away.

"Thane," she called out.

He stopped. Fear kept him from turning around, but it didn't stop her from talking.

"I...," she trailed off and he finally had the nerve to look at her. "I want you to know I love you."

He blinked rapidly, unsure if he heard her right.

"I know you don't love me and that's okay. I just wanted you to know that I love you, and I hope you find your happiness on Olympus." She turned away before he could say anything. The door closed with a hard thud and his heart sank.

Numbly he climbed into his car and drove home. Her words echoing in his head the entire way there.

CHAPTER THIRTEEN

January 31st - Early morning

"You're a dumbass." An all too familiar voice boomed, jolting Thane awake. He squinted at the clock next to his bed and realized he had only been asleep for a couple of hours.

"What the fuck do you want?"

Gabriel chuckled and opened the curtains, letting light cascade into the room. "It's time to rise and shine. Get your ass out of bed. And, is that any way to talk to the man bearing good news?"

"Fuck off, I'm not in the mood." A crackle of lightening sparked in the room, causing Thane to bolt up out of the bed. "What the fuck was that for?"

"Don't be a dickhead. Get your butt dressed. We need to talk." Gabriel stormed from the room; his heavy tread easy to hear descending the wooden stairs.

Sighing with annoyance, Thane threw on whatever clothes were closest. Belatedly, he realized he should have paid more attention. As he made his way downstairs, the soft scent of jasmine rose, tickling his nose.

Amara.

Ever since leaving her the day before, he'd missed her. He caught himself looking for her in his kitchen even though she'd never been there. He imagined she would be waiting in his bed, which was cold and lonely. He missed sitting out on the patio listening to the creatures of the night as she drifted off to sleep in his arms.

He fell in love and, for the first time in his life, he decided he couldn't be selfish.

It. Fucking. Sucked.

Gabriel greeted him with a cup of coffee in the living room. They each took a seat on the leather chairs, just as they always did.

Thane wasn't in the mood for whatever the man had to say. He figured out in the early hours of the dawn that nothing Gabriel said would make him happy…not even news of being allowed to return to Olympus. Only Amara would make him happy, and he was trying to do the right thing by her.

"Want to tell my why you're so pissy?" Gabriel asked over the rim of his cup.

Thane grunted and took a drink of the hot brew. Enjoying the scalding in his throat too much, because it made him feel something other than remorse.

Gabriel sighed heavily. "Fine. I'll get to the point. I can tell you won't be any fun today. Why didn't you tell her you loved her?"

Thane's eyebrow shot up in surprise. "So, you know then?"

His friend waved a dismissive hand. "Of course. We know everything, plus there is more at stake here than your return to Olympus."

103

"You could have told me that when you gave me the task," he groused.

Gabriel's features turned hard and cold. Someone would be hearing from the angry man if he went by that look. "I only recently found out."

Thane snorted. If there was one thing Gabriel and the rest of the Great Watchers didn't like, it was being used for an ulterior motive.

"Tell me why you kept your dumb mouth shut for once. She told you she loved you. It would have been the perfect time."

Thane studied his friend, for the first time since his banishment; the animosity and feeling of betrayal he usually felt weren't there. "Here's something that will turn that frown upside down, old friend."

Gabriel's dark eyebrow rose in question. It had to be a shock to hear Thane call him friend. It had been too many years since he had done that. Too many wasted years rebuffing the friendship the man offered.

"I didn't want to be selfish and make her feel like she had to give up her life and family to be with me."

"And you think she would have?"

"Yeah. But she has her clients to think of, and her brother has gone off the rails again. She wouldn't be happy being on Olympus with me while they were all here needing her help. I would be going back, wouldn't I?" Insecurity gripped him, and he was sure it came through in his voice.

Gabriel nodded, confirming what he guessed.

"Because I fell in love, I would be allowed home."

"Would it really be home if she isn't there? You have options, Thane, and it isn't a one or the other kind of deal. It would have to fall into what is planned, but I think you would be agreeable."

104

He hadn't thought about that. His heart for so long had been set on gaining entry back to Olympus. No other living arrangements had occurred to him. "What options?"

Gabriel chuckled lightly. His lips curved into a genuine grin of happiness. "You could stay here and she could move in or vice versa. Personally, I prefer her place. The gate provides additional security and, now that the brother has left, you can fill the upstairs with the next generation of Eternals and Angels. There are stipulations set by Zeus, though."

Thane glossed over the comment about Zeus. Whatever those were, he would deal with it later. The thought of filling a nursery appealed to him more than he thought it would. "What of Olympus and my brothers? It has been many years since I've seen them and I admit, I've missed them. Would I be able to visit? Could they come here? Would Amara be allowed to travel through the realms unharmed?"

"Yes, to all of it. Zeus wants Amara to partake in the Turning Ceremony. The ambrosia is strongest today, so you will need to decide quickly, as well as convince your love."

"Immortal? Then its what I figured. He wants her as a member of his realm. I can deal with that." He wouldn't have to watch her grow old and die. They could be together for all eternity. They would definitely be able to make those babies.

"Yes, then there is Zeus's stipulation beyond you falling in love. Amara is the daughter of the progeny of the Muse Clio; she is a twin as well as being an Eternal. She has the gift of time's history and that of understanding and guidance. Zeus wants her to be Persephone's companion when Persephone is on his realm. Amara's brother will find out much later that he is to be her companion in the Underworld. The twins connection will snap back into being once they are both in place."

"Holy shit." Thane sat back in his chair in shock. His

Amara was definitely a gift and not just to him.

"Indeed." Gabriel leaned back in his chair as well. Silence descended upon them as Thane tried to come to terms with all he had been told.

A question occurred to him. "Was that the 'more at stake' you mentioned before?"

"No. That is something else entirely. I cannot talk about it," he grumped. "Amara's fate has always been this. You falling in love was icing on the cake for them all. A way to bring you both into the fold."

Thane nodded in understanding. The large grandfather clock struck seven. Typically, at this time, Amara would be waking him up with sweet kisses and nibbles. Claiming she needed a taste of him to start the morning right.

"Are you ready to declare your love?" Gabriel asked, standing from his chair.

Thane looked up at his friend. A cock-sure grin lit Gabriel's face. He knew Thane's decision before he'd even made it. In the past, that would have pissed him off. Now, he couldn't be happier having a friend that knew him so well.

He stood and squared his shoulders. "Yeah. I'm ready to lay claim to my woman. She doesn't need those horny dogs on Olympus sniffing around her. I won't allow her to go there unattached and unprotected."

"Good." Gabriel's beefy hand landed on his shoulder. Next thing Thane knew, they were standing on Amara's front porch.

He swayed slightly on his feet. "Damn, I forgot what that felt like."

Gabriel's laughter reverberated off the walls, rattling the front door. Thane joined him. Allowing the joy to fill him.

They were both stunned into silence when Amara's door whipped open. Her thunderous expression quickly morphed into shock. "Thane," she breathed out softly. She looked at him with wonder in her eyes. When she scanned to his left and saw the man standing with him, the wonder turned to confusion. "Gabe?"

"Oh! Um…I meant to take off." He glanced around and disappeared right before their eyes.

"Coward," he murmured. Thane expected Amara to shriek at Gabriel's vanishing act but, as usual, she didn't. He would need to remember that not much surprised his love.

"Who are you calling a coward? You're the one who left without telling me you loved me."

Thane frowned. Grabbing her by the arm, he pulled her inside the house. He was torn between heading straight to the bedroom, having a conversation in the family room, or going outside to the patio where he felt at peace the most. Amara made the decision for him, yanking her arm from his grasp and walking to the kitchen. She poured a cup of coffee and cupped it in her hands. Leaning back against the counter she waited, her foot tapping with impatience.

Thane settled against the counter in front of her, arms crossed over his chest. "You're right. I'm a coward."

When he didn't say anything more, her nostrils flared. She was irritated, but that wasn't all. A burst of heat flashed in her eyes, telling him she wasn't as mad as she was acting. He smiled inside.

"And…" she said through gritted teeth.

"And I shouldn't have left like I did. I should have told you how I felt, but I didn't because I thought I was doing what was best for you."

Her shoulders slumped and she slid the coffee mug onto the counter. "No, doing what was best for me would have been talking to me and not letting me think you didn't love me. Doing what was best would have been giving me the options, the choice to decide what was best for me."

Thane couldn't take it anymore. Stepping forward, he pulled her into his arms. She clung to him, burying her face in his chest. "When did you figure it all out?"

"After you were gone and I cried a bucket of tears and wished death upon you, even though I knew that wouldn't happen. It finally dawned on me the second week you were in my house; you figured out what you needed to do in order to return home. Not once did you casually toss out that you loved me just to get your golden ticket. Not even when you left yesterday, breaking my heart."

She sniffled into his shirt. "Don't cry, little one." Stroking a hand down her back, he soothed her the best he could.

She was right. His intended selflessness hurt her more than the selfish act of begging her to go with him. Not once did he think beyond living in Olympus. Male stupidity was the only thing he could blame.

He tugged on her braid and smiled when she looked up at him. "I'm sorry, Amara. Nothing I can say will make up for me being an idiot."

She gave him a watery smile. "There's one thing."

"I love you, Amara. You're my every breath. My every thought. Without you, I'll never be the man I'm supposed to be."

"I love you too, Thane." She went up on her tiptoes, kissing him on his lips. He wouldn't tell anyone, but he swooned in that moment. The love of his life was in his arms, kissing him like he was the last man on earth.

Minutes passed before she dropped down to her feet. "We have a lot to work out," she said. Happiness shone in her eyes, and he knew there was nothing they couldn't conquer together. A little moving between realms would be nothing.

"We do, but first I think we should make love. I've missed you too damn much."

She chuckled as she threaded their fingers together. She pulled him out of the kitchen and they made their way to the bedroom. "You've only been gone one day."

"And that's one day too long." Sweeping her up in his arms, she giggled. They made it to her room, where he showed her how much he missed her for the rest of the day.

EPILOGUE

Chloe stood at the back of the Parthenon watching as Thane and Amara stepped forward towards Zeus. The woman was rather pretty. Dark hair. Warm caramel skin. Full lips and hauntingly beautiful whiskey-colored eyes. There was an aura around her that spoke of the old soul within. If Thane hadn't come through, she would have been plucked up quickly by some other man the second she stepped foot within the realm.

Chloe crossed her arms over her chest in satisfaction. It hadn't been difficult getting them to cross paths. A quick word with Gabriel, the randy Great Watcher she'd played with a time or two before, and her plan was set in motion. She would force them to meet. Put him right in the woman's path.

Caught up in thought, it took Chloe a moment to realize someone stood next to her. Tilting her head, she glanced to her right. "Eros," she said, her voice breathy. Too breathy as far as she was concerned. The long month of not seeing him, along with wondering what he was up to, played havoc with her, mentally and physically. More than she thought it would.

He stared ahead, not bothering to look at her. It irritated her on a level she didn't understand. She hated being ignored in general, but when it was from someone she was interested in, she saw red. In fact, it infuriated her that a man she desired for his body and couldn't stop thinking of was ignoring her.

"They make a lovely couple, don't you think?"

Chloe turned her head back to the couple. Amara was drinking ambrosia from a goblet, as Thane stood behind her. His snowy white wings were on display, curving forward in a show of protection. "She would have done well without him I'm sure."

"You're probably right, but there was more to their joining than meets the eye."

Her brow furrowed, head swiveling toward Eros. "Care to let me in on that?"

"It has nothing to do with the bet. Just know there was a stake in it for Zeus, and he is very pleased with the results."

"I would hear his thanks in person." She stepped forward but was stopped when his large hand gripped her arm. He pulled her back, forcing her to face him.

"You will not. Zeus is aware we have a bet, but not about with whom we are playing. He would have my head if he knew I used an Eternal and Girgori as your first challenge."

"Then why use them at all if it was that important?"

Eros shrugged. "I'd say their joining was, what is that term humans are fond of — a gimme."

The slow burn of anger began beneath her skin. He thought to take it easy on her. Did he see this bet as a joke? "I do not need you to go easy on me, Eros. Anything you can do, I can do as well, if not better. Getting those two," she waved her hand in the direction of Thane and his woman, "together was a simple matter of timing and enchantment. A child could have done that."

His golden eyebrow lifted. "Bumping into her while in Viral City. You call that getting the job done?"

"I did what I felt needed to be done. There was no better opportunity. You would have done the same."

"But I am a man. You were reckless, Chloe. Anything could have happened to you." While the words came out calm, she sensed an underlying thread of anger.

Chloe narrowed her eyes and studied Eros. His jaw was clenched, a practiced smile on his face. A small, barely noticeable, tick formed in his jaw. The shock of what she was seeing smacked her in the face and made her heart race.

"You cannot tell me you were concerned for my well-being? That would go against everything I know about you." It would also mean he was more invested in her than he'd let her believe.

His nostrils flared and a flash of surprise crossed his face, which was quickly replaced with a devil-may-care grin. "It was only an observation. I'm sure you can take care of yourself."

She snorted and rolled her eyes. He could say what he wanted, but she knew he was concerned. Just the thought made her giddy. The dizzying feeling pulled the corners of her lips up into a smile. "If you say so. Now, about the next couple, I do hope you have something better."

Eros's jaw clenched before it relaxed. Gone was the concern that lit his green eyes, replaced by his typical blasé attitude. "Not tonight. I am here to enjoy the festivities of the Turning Ceremony. I'll see you tomorrow, my sweet Chloe."

For a split second, she thought he was going to lean

down and kiss her. She was wrong. He tipped his head and walked away. The throng of people around them swallowed him up. Turning on heel, Chloe left. She didn't intend on sticking around to see him find another woman to spend the evening with.

THE END

Parvati: February
Mystic Zodiac, Book 2

TEZ Publishing

Parvati Shiva, a true descendent of the Goddess of love and devotion, is fed up. She runs a successful dating site, connecting Mystics and humans all over the world with their one true love. The only she hasn't been able to find love for is…her.

When a hacker gets into her network and website, shutting down her site in the height of the busy season, she calls on her cousin Jag for help, who in turn reaches out to an old friend.

Colin Patterson, IT guru and confirmed bachelor, quickly agrees to help his friend's sister out with her computer problem, hoping it will be a long drawn out process. He's eager to escape his mother's matchmaking Valentine's Day party. She's invited all of the single women—and a few men—to jump-start his dating life, something he has no interest in at all.

One mistaken identity later, Colin ruins his chance with the beautiful Indian woman he's instantly attracted to. Will he be able to prove he isn't a boss bashing idiot, save Parvati's company, and win her affections before he doesn't have a reason to stick around?

Warning: This book contains a geeky hero who can't keep his mouth shut, a strong willed businesswoman dealing in love, and an attraction that neither can deny.

Please note: **This book has a hot M/M scene.**

Word Count: 26,817

EXCERPT:

"No, no, no!" Parvati smashed the keys on her keyboard; hoping one of them would stop the pop-ups decorating her screen. Her computer display froze for a second before a new single box popped up in the middle. "You're drunk. Go home. No one wants to date you." The giant laughing emoticon that followed filling up the screen pushed her over the edge. Picking up her mouse, she threw it across the room, watching with no sense of satisfaction as it pinged off the wall.

Why couldn't that have made her feel better? "Fucking technology," she growled. Not that she didn't love all things techie; she did, just not at the moment.

Stacy, her assistant, poked her head into the room. "I see you've found out." She squeezed through the barely open door, hands clasped in front of her demurely. She chewed on her lips nervously, and Parvati knew right then she wasn't going to like what would come out of Stacy's mouth.

"Why didn't you tell me when I walked in this morning?" She knew she sounded whiney but didn't care. This was the last thing she needed at the moment.

"I wasn't aware of the problem until Jag called."

Squeezing her eyes shut tight, Parvati counted back from ten.

10...

9...

8...

She would have put her hands over her ears to keep from hearing anything, but that would have been childish and not the behavior of the head of a thriving Internet dating company.

7…

6…slowly breathe in and out. Find your center. Her therapist's voice echoed words of advice in her head. The soothing tone doing nothing for her at the moment.

"We've been hacked. At least that's what Jag says. He told me to tell you he's bringing someone in to help find, fix, and contain the problem. He's not sure when that will be though. He has to get hold of the whoever this technical guru is and see if he's free first."

Stacy's words jolted her from her countdown. Her therapist told her it would help her relax and think clearly. Boy was she wrong. That bitch wasn't getting her repeat business.

Parvati groaned and dropped her head to the keyboard in defeat, banging it lightly. One more thing to go wrong that day—she should have just stayed in bed. It started shitty and looked like it would end shitty.

Mother-fuck!

When the heel on her favorite pair of shoes snapped as she walked out her front door, she should have just turned around, stripped naked, and crawled back under the covers until the day came to an end.

Nope. Not her. Not Ms. I-have-to-impress-the-boss-or-he'll-fire-me. She trudged on even though she had an inkling things wouldn't get better. She tossed the shoes and grabbed another pair. Luckily, she made it to her favorite teashop without incident. Unluckily for her, her tea got knocked over before she even had a chance to take a sip. The busy mom with the three rambunctious kids bumping into her as she walked out the teashop door.

To top off her morning, the asshat she went on a blind date

with earlier in the month hand-delivered a wedding invitation, and thanked her for proving the gossip right.

Now there was…THIS. Hacked! Who would want to hack a dating website? She knew the answer before she even finished the thought. A supremely disgruntled customer or rejected suitor. The ratio of displeased customers and suitors was minimal when compared to happy clients. But the rejects—they were really unhappy. Hate mail. Social media bashing. Failed cyber attacks. Unfortunately, in this business, there would always be a match that didn't work out, and they would always have to deal with the aftermath. This time, Parvati wasn't sure she could handle it.

Stacy's voice filtered through the myriad of thoughts circling in her head.

"Sweetie, you might want to stop that or the space bar will be permanently etched into your forehead. How would that go over on your date tonight?"

Gideon: March
Mystic Zodiac, Book 3

TEZ Publishing

Gideon Deckard is finally getting a little time away from the Keystone Predator Pack to go wolf. All he has planned is a week of running wild through the Grand Canyon before the hiking season starts back up. Once it does, he'll go back to what he does best…being the Alpha he was born to be.

Ryder Sparks can barely contain her excitement. She's taking a week off from work at the family store, Sparks Sporting & Outdoors, and going on her dream vacation. A four day hiking trip on a lesser traveled trek through the Grand Canyon. The season has opened early and she was the first to get the coveted pass. She's looking forward to pushing herself on her first solo trip and discovering who she was really meant to be.

A run in with a massive grey wolf has Ryder stumbling and getting knocked out. When she wakes up, she's back in her tent and there's a hunky man there to help her get back on her feet. When she finds out he's a wolf-shifter instead of freaking out, she decides to go on the adventure of a lifetime with him. Now all she has to do is convince Gideon to give her a chance to be his one and only Luna.

Word Count: 36,270

EXCERPT:

March 9 ~ 8am

Ryder practically bounced out of her Jeep, as she
pulled to a stop at the Backcountry Information
Center. It was odd for them to ask someone to pick
up their permit in person, but she didn't mind. For
months she'd planned this trip, making sure she did
everything by the book to get the highly sought-
after paper. The hardest part was waiting for the
exact minute she could fax in her application. The
backpacking permit she wanted was one of the
hardest permits to get in the national park system,
and she was determined to get one.

Four, possibly five, days of hiking and camping
in the Grand Canyon on a solo trip, going from
Grandview Point to the South Kaibab Trail. It was the
best present she'd ever given herself.

Not that her roommate would agree with that. Pansy
thought she was crazy for wanting to spend time
walking around a — as she put it — "super old bunch
of rocks." Pansy wasn't an outdoors kind of girl,
which was funny because she was a fox-shifter.

To Ryder it sounded like heaven. She'd grown up
hiking and camping with her family. Her love of the
outdoors inherently ingrained into her soul. Nothing
would ever take its place.

A woman in a green ranger outfit appeared in front
of the doors. She unlocked it and waved Ryder
forward. Ryder made sure she got there precisely
when they opened. Hopefully it wouldn't take long,

and she would get back in time for her shift at the store. She counted herself lucky that her boss was forgiving. It also didn't hurt that he was her dad. He knew her plans for the trip, and she'd called to let him know she had to pick up her permit.

The rangers probably wanted to make sure she could handle the solo trip. A lot of people mistook her for being younger than her twenty-four years. She attributed it to her healthy lifestyle and lack of sitting behind a desk.

She breezed into the building, making a beeline for the brunette ranger from before. A golden-haired man stood near her, and there was a strange undercurrent between them. Like a sexual tension neither wanted to acknowledge.

Not my problem. She shrugged and approached the desk. "Hi, I'm Ryder Sparks. I got a call about picking up my backcountry permit. I was told I had to get it today."

The female ranger looked at her and smiled. "Sure thing, hon." The southern twang that came out of her mouth threw Ryder off. She didn't looked like a Southerner. There was something almost ethereal about her. The blond fellow snickered, and the woman shot a glare his way.

"Okay," Ryder said under breath, dragging the word out. There was definitely something going on between the pair. When the woman just stood there glaring at the man, Ryder decided to move things along. "So, the permit?"

"Oh." The woman turned and blindly grabbed some paperwork. She slid it across the countertop, and Ryder was surprised to see it was actually hers. "If I can get you to sign here and here," she pointed to two places without looking down, "I'll get you on your way."

"Thanks." Ryder snatched up the pen and was about to sign; she stopped and looked up at the woman. "Don't you need to see my ID or anything? Make sure I'm the person this paper says I am."

"Now, honey, why would anyone come in claiming to

be someone they aren't for a four-day backcountry permit?" The southern drawl dripped from her lips, grating against Ryder's ears. "Besides darlin', you look like that picture you faxed in."

Ryder's brows furrowed. The woman hadn't even looked at the paperwork...but whatever. "Okay then." She signed quickly and pushed the paper back across the counter. The woman handed it to the man and picked up another slip of paper. She rubbed her fingers over it and cocked her head to the side. She nibbled on her lip, then cast a glance at the man, who drew up closer. "This is the right one, isn't it Cup... uh, Cupert?"

Cupert (and what a shitty name that must have been growing up) snatched the paper from her hand. He ran his fingers over it just like she did, then handed it to Ryder. "Looks to be. Here ya' go."

"Uh, thanks." Reaching out, she took it from the frowning man. The second her fingers touched it she felt a spark. Goosebumps rose on her flesh, and a shiver tripped down her spine.

"Make sure you don't lose it, and remember to clip it to your tent when camping." The man pushed over some brochures, which Ryder grabbed.

"Was there anything else?" Ryder looked between the rangers, fully expecting a lecture or something. There had to be a reason they wanted her to drive all the way from Flagstaff to pick the permit up.

"Nope," the man said, he looked bored and ready to escape already.

"No reason why I needed to drive an hour to come in here to get this? It isn't normal practice, or did something change?"

The woman shrugged and looked at Cupert.

He rolled his eyes, "Just doing what we're told. We

don't make the rules, just enforce them."

"Humph, okay then. Thanks." Ryder spun on her heel and headed toward the door.

"Y'all come back and see us sometime now, ya' hear." The woman's voice rang out and stopped Ryder in her tracks. She looked over her shoulder and saw the brunette's big bubbly grin. Cupert snickered behind her back, earning a smack from the woman.

"Sure," she said noncommittally, and slid through the doors as they swooshed open in front of her. "I think they've been out in the wild too long," she murmured, as the doors closed behind her.

Hopping into her Jeep, she took a few seconds to look at her permit. The itinerary was printed on it; along with advisories for the area she would be in. The thing that thrilled her most—her name across the bottom: Sparks, Ryder.

She couldn't stop the squeal that escaped her lips. Revving up the Jeep, she tore out of the parking lot. One more week and she would be on the trip of a lifetime.

Currently available in ebook only

Shifted Plans
Shifter U, Book 1

Decadent Publishing

Avery Hillman has one year of college left. Once it's over she has plans, BIG plans. A job managing her family's medical practice, an apartment of her own, and a new life where she's the one in charge. No hovering family, no annoying siblings, and no mate to have to divide her time to be with.

Declan Weller has one more class to finish. One more thing he can cross off his ten-year plan. Once that is done, he can transfer to the new job waiting for him and his new life. He isn't looking for his mate and as far as he's concerned, finding her can wait another two years.

The Fates have a plan of their own. One that includes throwing Avery and Declan in each other's path. It's high time those two found each other and learn the most important thing of all...sometimes plans need to shift.

~~~~~

Genre: Paranormal Romance, New Adult, Shifters
Featuring Lion Shifters

Word Count: 27,796

Available in ebook and print

Craving More
Tiger Nip, Book 1

TEZ Publishing

Corrine Hart is ready for few days off for rest and relaxation.
At the top of her to-do list is spending as much time as possible in tiger form and doing her best to banish all thoughts
of the mysterious Hunky Cupcake Guy who spent the last
two weeks driving her libido insane.

Jett Montgomery-Murphy just wants to know if the tasty
treats that keep showing up at work are the same ones his
best friend used to get while they were in college. A trip out
to Sweet Confections confirms what he thought and brings
him in close contact with the one woman he's secretly lusted
after for years, his best friend's sister Corrine.

A late night tryst leads to two tigers finding their mates and
two humans unsure what to do next. Add in an overbear-
ing brother, a best friend with her own drama, and a crazy
ex-girlfriend that has a checkered past and you have a recipe
for disaster.

Will Corrine and Jett be able to overcome the unexpected
obstacles on their way to falling in love? Or will they throw
in the towel before the relationship even gets off the ground?

~~~~~
Genre: Paranoraml Romance, Shifters
Featuring Tiger Shifter

*Word Count: 47,309*

## Claiming More
Tiger Nip, Book 2

TEZ Publishing

Sampson Hart has known Mary Jane Poppy for ten years. She's his sister's best friend, business partner, and has had a crush on Sam for years. When the mating pull hits him, he's ready to claim her as his own. Given their history, it should be simple. Right?

MJ has loved Sam since she was fifteen. But being a hybrid, she's been told all her life she won't have a mate. When Sam proclaims she belongs to him, she doesn't believe it; the mating pull isn't there, and Sam isn't meant to be hers.

Running back home to escape the love she feels for Sam, MJ agrees to become the companion of a man who lost his mate and has three young children to raise. It is the only way to set Sam free to find the one he is truly meant to be with.

Will Sam be Claiming More or will the one he desires the most find comfort in the arms of another?

~~~~~

Genre: Paranoraml Romance, Shifters
Featuring Tiger Shifter

Word Count: 58,101

B
O
N
U
S

Available in ebook and print

Dallas & Kacie: Tiger Bite
Tiger Nip, Book 2.5

TEZ Publishing

It's the holiday season and Kacie Cook is counting down the hours until its time to close up Sweet Confections. Not that she has any great plans for the week the bakery is closed. She won't be seeing her family — yet again, and all of her friends are too busy. All she has planned is a little rest and relaxation. That is until the last customer of the night walks in. Could he be the one to bring some holiday cheer and possibly change her life forever?

~~~~~

Genre: Paranoraml Romance, Shifters
Featuring Tiger Shifter

Word Count: 15,773

ABOUT THE AUTHOR

Brandy is a paranormal romance author who, on occasion, likes to dabble with contemporary. She's addicted to MDK shows and who-done-its. You'll almost never see her without some type of skull paraphernalia on and is always dreaming of more tattoos.

Brandy is a Navy brat, prior enlisted Army, current Army wife, and mom. She lives in Virginia with her husband of almost 20 years, their three kids and one dog.

Brandy is all over the web. Pick one or all to keep up with her.

Don't forget to sign up for the newsletter. There is a monthly giveaway and when the mood strikes other fun things like deep discounts in the shop.

www.brandywalker.net

facebook.com/BrandyWalkerfanpage

twitter.com/Brandy_W

OTHER BOOKS BY BRANDY WALKER

TEZ PUBLISHING

Tiger Nip

Craving More, Book 1

Claiming More, Book 2

Dallas & Kacie: Tiger Bite, Book 2.5

Finding More, Book 3 (future release)

Giving More, Book 4 (future release)

Seeing More, Book 5 (future release)

Freefall

Caught in the Moment, Book 1

Fly Guy Next Door, Book 2

Captured by Color, Book 3 (future release)

Revving Her Engine, Book 4 (future release)

Spinning Out of Control, Book 5 (future release

Mystic Zodiac

Thane | January | Angel

Parvati | February | God/Goddess

Gideon | March | Shifter

Lisa | April | Nymph (releasing Apr 2015)

Celeste | May | Fae (releasing May 2015)

Willow | June | Witch/Warlock (releasing Jun 2015)

Amber | July | Siren (releasing Jul 2015)

Adrian | August | Dragon (releasing Aug 2015)

Colby | September | Djinn (releasing Sep 2015)

Lucas | October | Vampire (releasing Oct 2015)

Mace | November | Spirit (releasing Nov 2015)

Falcon | December | Demon (releasing Dec 2015)

B
O
N
U
S

Keystone Predators

Under Her Spell (releasing Jun 2015)

Praetorian Guards

New series in the works

DECADENT PUBLISHING

ROAR LINE

Shifter U

Shifted Plans, Book 1

Changing Her Tune, Book 2 (future release)